MAC'S DESTINY

Charon MC
Book 8

KHLOE WREN

Books by Khloe Wren

Charon MC:
Inking Eagle
Fighting Mac
Chasing Taz
Claiming Tiny
Chasing Scout
Tripping Nitro
Scout's Legacy
Mac's Destiny

Fire and Snow:
Guardian's Heart
Noble Guardian
Guardian's Shadow
Fierce Guardian
Necessary Alpha
Protective Instincts

Dragon Warriors:
Enchanting Eilagh
Binding Becky
Claiming Carina
Seducing Skye
Believing Binda

Jaguar Secrets:
Jaguar Secrets
FireStarter

Other Titles:
Fireworks
Tigers Are Forever
Bad Alpha Anthology
Scarred Perfection
Scandals: Zeck
Mirror Image Seduction
Deception
Mine To Bear

ISBN: 978-0-6483085-9-1
Copyright © Khloe Wren 2019

Cover Credits:
Model: Alfie Gordillo
Photographer: Reggie Deanching of R+M Photography
Digital Artist: Khloe Wren
Editing Credits:
Editor: Carolyn Depew of Write Right

Acknowledgements

For the second time in this series, I've found myself writing a second book for a couple. Neither of these books were something I saw coming, but I'm so happy they have. I loved writing more of Scout and Marie, and now I've got to enjoy giving you all another slice of Mac and Zara's life. I aimed to write this book in such a way that even if you haven't read Fighting Mac, you won't get lost reading this.

As with all my books, I couldn't have written it without the support of my wonderful husband and daughters. My eldest really stepped up to help out around the house so I could get this one finished.

I suspect at this point, Claudia Bost regrets letting me know she works in an ER. Lol, but I really appreciate all the times she's helped me with medical research. I hope your daughter likes the introduction to Sparrow in this story.

To my editor, Carolyn, no matter what I throw at you, you always come through with a marvelous edit. And just for something different, this one wasn't completely last minute and a rush job! I appreciate everything you do and thank you for another job well done.

To my PA Andrea Rhoads, thank you for keeping me sane and doing all you do to make my life easier so I can focus on writing. My fb sprint group, the Night Writers, thank you all for the many, many sprints that got this baby done. To my street team, thank you for the support.
xo
Khloe Wren

Biography

Khloe Wren grew up in the Adelaide Hills before her parents moved the family to country South Australia when she was a teen. A few years later, Khloe moved to Melbourne which was where she got her first taste of big city living.

After a few years living in the big city, she missed the fresh air and space of country living so returned to rural South Australia. Khloe currently lives in the Murraylands with her incredibly patient husband, two strong willed young daughters, and an ever growing list of animals.

As a child Khloe often had temporary tattoos all over her arms. When she got her first job at 19, she was at the local tattooist in the blink of an eye to get her first real tattoo. Khloe now has four, two taking up much of her back.

While Khloe doesn't ride a bike herself, she loves riding pillion behind her husband on the rare occasion they get to go out without their daughters.

Dedication

To Andrea Rhoads

Author Note

The heroine of this book, Zara, suffers with the medical condition Narcolepsy.

Recently, they've classed Narcolepsy into two types. Type 1 has two major symptoms: day time sleeping and Cataplexy (sudden onset of muscle weakness that may be precipitated by excitement or emotion), while Type 2 doesn't have Cataplexy. Zara suffers from Type 1 Narcolepsy.

As with most medical conditions, no two cases of Narcolepsy are the same. Zara's symptoms are based heavily on a friend who has Type 1 Narcolepsy (with Cataplexy). I did that on purpose, as I wanted to make Zara as realistic as possible. Please keep in mind, however, that this story is a work of fiction and there are times where things get exaggerated from what is considered normal. Also, just because Zara reacts a certain way to a particular situation, it's not to say that every sufferer of this condition will react that way.

Charon:

Char·on \ˈsher-ən, ˈker-ən, -än\

In Greek mythology, the Charon is the ferryman who takes the dead across either the river Styx or Acheron, depending on whether the soul's destination is the Elysian Fields or Hades.

Chapter 1

Mac

More than happy to be back on home soil, I sat in my usual spot next to Eagle and Taz as Scout called church to order. This wasn't our usual weekly meeting, but a special one so Scout could fill in the rest of the club in on what had happened up north.

What a fucking mess that had turned out to be. We'd gone up there in order to find a way to put a stop to the Ice Riders, an MC up in Boston, after they sent two of their men down here after us. Fuckers decided to get our attention by holding a gun on Scout's pregnant old lady. Yeah, the Ice Riders had been a clever bunch of bastards.

When we'd arrived in New York, we'd found so much more going on than just our issues with the Ice Riders. We'd called ahead and thought we'd arranged to stay with the Satan Knights MC while we did our thing. That would have been fucking great except for the fact that when Scout had called Jack Parrish, the man hadn't mentioned he wasn't the president anymore, and had walked away from the club. Not only that, he and the club had shit going down with a fucking cartel. Ironically, it had been the same cartel causing problems for the Ice Riders.

In the end, we somehow managed to have it work out that all the Charons and Satan's Knights were still standing, while the Ice Riders MC was nothing more than a cautionary tale on why you don't mess with either of our clubs. Also sent a damn strong message out to other MCs that might think they could take on the Charon MC because we were a single-chapter club. We had friends, powerful ones, ones who had our backs and if you came after us, fucked with us or our families, they would help us come for you and vengeance would be delivered. Once we had the Ice Riders dealt with, we didn't hang around. Wolf, the Knights' new president, had assured us they had things with the cartel under control and we could head on home to our families.

Listening to Scout recap everything made it hard to believe how so much shit went down in the few short days we were up north, and I was there for it. It wouldn't surprise me if some of the others didn't believe it.

"So, the Ice Riders are history and gone for good. The Satan's Knights are still our allies, with Wolf now holding the gavel. That leaves one more enemy we need to take care of to truly end this shit for good."

As Scout finished talking, his gaze found mine. And stayed there. Dammit.

"Antonio Sabella. We need to vote on sending a crew over to deal with that fucker once and for all. All in favor?"

Sounded like every man in the room uttered a response.

"All against?"

Dead, fucking silence.

"Fuck."

I uttered the curse as I realized what my club president was about to say. Sabella was a mob boss out in L.A. A man I'd gotten information on in the past. Everyone in this room knew I'd be the best option to send after the bastard.

I'd missed my girls something fierce while I'd been away, and now it looked like I wasn't going to be getting much quality time with them before I was going to have to leave again, which sucked. My old lady, Zara, who was fucking perfect and I loved more than life, was going to be mad as hell. She had a couple of medical issues—narcolepsy and cataplexy—that made her nervous when she was alone with our daughter, especially overnight.

Strange thing was, since she'd had Cleo, she'd been doing better. It was like her maternal instinct overrode the illnesses somehow. If Cleo needed her mom, Zara was there, on it. But it didn't stop Zara from being filled with all the what ifs. Like, what if she was holding Cleo and had a cataplexy attack and dropped her when she went down? Or, what if she was struggling with her narcolepsy and couldn't get out of bed when our girl needed something? I was confident those things would never happen, but she wasn't. So she preferred it when I was there with her, especially at night.

I fought the grin that wanted to break free at the thought of what else Zara liked about me being home with her. Especially at night, after Cleo was tucked into bed. Fuck, two years later and I still couldn't get enough of my wife. I mentally shook the thoughts free, trying to focus back on Scout and what I knew he was about to ask me to do.

Life sure had been simpler before I had a family of my own. I would have jumped at going on this run if I'd still been single. But I wasn't, and honestly, I wouldn't change my life for the world. Zara and Cleo owned me, heart and soul, and I wouldn't have it any other way. I just wished I could find a way to be by their sides 24/7 and still accomplish everything else that needed to be done.

"Mac, you did real good up north, brother. Everyone's impressed. I wish I could give you a week off before I send you out again, but we don't have that kind of time. Sabella will hear about what happened up north and know we're going to come for him. We need to strike now, before he's got time to plan. And, brother, you're the only one of us with the contacts in L.A. to get this shit done. Arrow will go with you again, along with Jazz. Need you to choose two others to go as well. And, brother? Don't think you won't be rewarded for all your hard work once this shit is done."

Ignoring that last, cryptic line and what it might mean, I focused on who I wanted to take with me. I glanced to my right, at Eagle and Taz. Not only were they both my club brothers, they'd also had my six in the USMC before we'd even heard of the Charon MC. Eagle gave me a firm nod, but Taz hesitated for the first time in our lives before he nodded. And I understood his hesitation. His daughter, Lolly, was only three months old. So while I appreciated that he'd still step up for me, I wasn't going to let him this time.

"Taz, you need to sit this one out, brother. Flick and Lolly need you to be here."

His eyes blazed. "Fuck that. I'm at your six, that's where I belong."

I tried to stare him down. Times like this, it would be nice if we were still in the USMC, me as their Gunnery Sergeant, since he and Eagle had to fucking listen to me. But here in the club? The three of us were all on equal ground.

"Mac's right, brother. We need you to stay close to home."

Scout spoke up and I watched as Taz clenched both his fists along with his jaw a moment before he dropped his head forward. Scout was our president and his word was law. Taz was staying home. I wrapped a hand around his shoulder.

"Times change, brother. Family comes first. We're not alone anymore. You not being there doesn't mean I'm not covered this time. And it means you can watch over Zara and Cleo for me."

His shoulders rose and fell with a deep breath before

he looked up, locking his gaze with mine. "I'll keep the home front guarded, brother."

I gave him a nod before releasing him and looking around at the rest of my club brothers.

"I want Eagle and…" My gaze traveled to each face, discounting each one for various reasons until I stopped. "Bank? You wanna come with? Get yourself outta town for a while?"

Poor bastard was having a time of it with his woman. I was pretty sure he'd jump at an excuse to leave town temporarily. That, and I'd seen the man in action. I knew he was solid in both hand-to-hand and with his firearms.

"Sure, brother. I've got your back."

Scout nodded. "Done. I've already spoken to Keys, and he and Donna will stay at your place. Help Zara with Cleo while you're gone. They'll also help Eagle, keeping an eye on Silk and Raven, too. I promise you, we'll take care of your families while you do this for the club. Hopefully it won't take long, then we can get back to what we should be about. Brotherhood and riding free. We need to vote in some new patch holders, celebrate what's good about this life instead being so fucking bogged down in protecting it we forget what the fuck we're protecting."

Cheers went up at that, but my heart was heavy. I loved being part of the club, would always do what was needed of me. And I appreciated that Scout had already thought to have Keys and Donna, who was a nurse, stay with my woman. But fuck it all, I'd only just gotten back after being away. I wanted a fucking minute to spend with my woman and daughter.

"When do we roll out? Wouldn't mind at least tonight to spend with my girls."

Scout gave another nod. "Done. This can wait till morning. But we need to plan." He hit the gavel on the table, ending church. "Everyone not heading west, get outta here."

I nodded to each of the men who gave my shoulder a slap and murmured words of encouragement on their way out. The whole while I kept my gaze on the Charon MC logo that hung on the wall behind the officers' table, wondering how the hell I ended up where I was. If someone had told me five years ago, this is where'd I'd land, I would have laughed in their face before asking what drugs they were on.

It had been a hell of a ride to get where I was currently standing. Being trusted to lead a second run within days of the first, which, considering Taz, Eagle and I had originally been sent here by the FBI to spy on the club, was amazing. The fact the club had allowed any of us to even stay in town after we were discovered was a miracle it itself.

Between our FBI handler turning out to be dirty, and us discovering that we actually liked being part of the Charon MC, we'd decided fairly early on to tell the feds to go fuck themselves. Didn't hurt that all three of us had found our women here in Bridgewater. But we hadn't come clean with Scout or the club about our FBI connections. We'd all hoped it would just vanish into the past, never to be seen again.

We really should have known better.

It all came out after the feds sent in Flick to get Taz back on their side. Of course, that shit backfired on the feds too. Flick was now married to Taz and no longer working for the FBI.

When Scout and the other officers had discovered the truth behind why Flick, the boys, and I were here, shit got real and could have easily ended with all four of us in the ground. But instead, they were now trusting me to lead the charge against this latest threat to our club. That meant a lot to me. I didn't give a fuck about whatever Scout had planned to reward me with. His trust, and that of the club, was enough.

While in New York, we'd discovered that it had been Antonio Sabella who'd told the Ice Riders MC they needed to come down and deal with us for him to forgive their debt to him. Stupid bastards choose to do that by holding a gun to the pregnant belly of Marie, Scout's old lady. She'd been eight months along and the shock of it had sent her into early labor. Thankfully, both Marie and little Joey were okay.

The Ice Riders MC were now nothing more than a footnote in Boston's history. Together with the Satan's Knights, we'd blown their shit to pieces, leaving no one standing. Now it was Sabella's turn, and despite the fact I hated leaving Zara and Cleo again so soon, I couldn't wait to go end that piece of shit for all he'd done to those

I cared about.

This latest stunt wasn't the first time the bastard had set his sights on the Charon MC, and is sure as fuck wasn't the first time I'd crossed paths with him. Sabella and I had a long history. After my sister had been murdered by her gang banger boyfriend, Sabella had come in and given me a way to get vengeance on her killer. I'd been so young and filled with rage, I'd jumped at the chance to take that fucker and his buddies down for what they'd put my sweet Bea through. I'd even been grateful to him for a long time. Until I figured out that he'd taken advantage of the situation to get me under his thumb and a rival gang leader taken care of. Once I calmed down from my rage and saw the bigger picture, I took the only way out I could find. Military service. Not even Sabella could argue with Uncle Sam.

Then, a few years back, he'd come gunning for Silk, Eagle's old lady. Silk's father had screwed with him, stripping him of money and information before he'd died in the 9/11 attack in New York. Unlucky for Silk, her father's bag containing the stolen information had missed his flight and it had taken LAX fifteen fucking years to discover it. Despite the time lapse, Sabella still wanted that bag and he'd come gunning for Silk so she could get it for him.

So, yeah, there was some serious fucking history between us, and along with the club, I was more than ready to end the association. Lately, I'd gotten the impression that my contact in L.A., who had been feeding me information about Sabella for years, was about done with sitting back and watching too, so hopefully he'd be ready to help us out with finishing off the fucker.

"Right, let's make this fast so we can all get back to our families, yeah?"

We all shifted so we sat in seats around the table, making it easier to hear each other. Scout waited for us to all get settled before he spoke again.

"Like when we went after Silk, I want this done on the sly. No colors. We don't want anyone to know we're there until we want them to see us. Ideally, I'd like him left dead in California, but if you have to bring him back with you, do it and we'll deal with it."

I shifted in my seat, getting everyone's attention.

"I need to talk to my guy before we go planning too much. I'll call him in a bit and see what's going on. Sabella stirred shit with the Ice Riders intentionally, so he's gotta expect some blow back from us. There's no point in us just blindly riding into town if we don't even know where the fucker is. Let me get a read on the situation, then we'll finalize a plan."

Scout gave me a nod. "Sounds good. Go check in with your woman, then make your call. We'll just hang out here till you get back, so don't take too long, yeah?"

Zara

My heart rate kicked up a notch as each man that wasn't mine came out of the meeting room. Mac had only just returned from heading up north, and I wanted him by my side already. The club had taken their turn, now it was mine, dammit.

Cleo, my ten month old daughter, whined and tugged at her ear. Again. Which pulled my complete attention away from the door and Mac to her sad, little face. I sighed. Looked like my daughter was coming down with something. Since she'd started crawling, I was normally having to chase her all over the damn place. Especially now she was pulling herself up and trying to walk. I loved my little girl to the moon and back, but she was a spitfire and on the go 24/7. So the fact she was actually wanting to sit in my lap and cling was unusual. Add in the ear rubbing she was doing and I knew something was off. I suspected—hoped—it was just another tooth coming in, and prayed it wouldn't be bad enough to keep her awake tonight. I had plans for her daddy and me.

Normally we women didn't get told much at all about the *club business* that went on, but the fact I'd been with Marie when those bastards had come in with guns out, made it hard to keep us out of the loop this time. Also, the grim expressions on the faces of the men when they'd returned from up north were a fairly good indicator that what they'd had to do hadn't been pretty. Or legal, no doubt. But I also had complete confidence the club had made it so there wouldn't be any more Ice Riders coming after us, and all our guys who went out had come home, so as far as I was concerned, it was a good day.

"Wonder what that's all about?"

As Flick, who was sitting next to me, with her three month old daughter, Lolly, asleep in her arms, spoke, I looked up to see the door close before Mac or Eagle had come through. Flick's man, Taz, had come out but hadn't looked happy as he'd stormed off to the bar.

"No clue, but it looks like it's something that involves Mac and Eagle, but not Taz."

As I'd spoken, Silk had come and flopped down in a seat next to us. With Bulldog out of church, her one year old son, Raven, was all over Grandpa, giving Silk a moment to relax.

"Try not to stress too much over it. Club shit blows over as fast as it blows up most of the time. And we know our men are good at what they do."

Silk was not only Eagle's old lady, she was the niece to the VP, Bulldog. She'd grown up in the club since she came to live with her uncle and aunt as a teen. Flick and I were new to all this club stuff. Neither of us had any idea of what we were getting tangled up in when we'd met and fallen for our men. Well, Flick had been an undercover FBI agent, so she'd known a little. But I'd grown up in Galveston, and down there everyone knew you stayed far away from the Iron Hammers, the local MC that ruled the town.

I'd been on a steep learning curve since hooking up with Mac, but for the most part, club life was great. It was basically this always-growing family that was somewhat dysfunctional, but always had your back. It did get a little dangerous at times, which sucked, but as I'd learned before settling in with the Charons, life could be dangerous. Didn't matter who you were.

The door to the meeting room opened again and this time Mac was the only one out of the door before it closed again. The fact Cleo stayed clinging to me as he came striding over to us was another indicator she wasn't well. My girl was definitely one-hundred percent a daddy's girl, except when she was sick. Then she was all about barfing all over Mommy, not Daddy.

"Hey, bunny. I gotta make a call, then head back in with the others. But after that we can go home." He stroked his hand over Cleo's hair with concern in his gaze.

"She's probably just teething. She'll be fine, babe. Go do what you gotta do."

Even if it turned out to not be a new tooth, I was worried enough for both of us, and clearly there was still club business that he needed to handle. If it was anything like the shit that had happened in the past, it would need his full attention. The last thing I wanted was for him to get shot or stabbed, or to come off his bike because he was stressing over Cleo or me. So, I'd be a good old lady and fake that everything was sunshine and fucking rainbows until he was done and came back to me.

After a quick peck on my lips and a kiss to Cleo's temple, he turned and headed off down the hallway to where the offices were.

Silk bumped her shoulder into mine, which had Cleo tightening her grip as she rubbed her cheek against my chest on a moan.

"Damn. Sorry, Cleo. Didn't mean to jostle you, baby. Look at those rosy cheeks. You think she's cutting another tooth?"

"Yeah, I'm hoping that's all it is. I'm that stressed out already, I really don't want to add her being sick to the mix."

I'd taken extra meds this morning to try to stay with it tonight, but I could feel the tiredness of my narcolepsy pulling me down. I hoped Mac didn't take too long. I'd been counting on getting a little couple time before I passed out on him.

"If you need to head home now, I can give you a ride. Raven can hang out with the men till they come home later."

My eyes stung with the threat of tears at her kindness. I'd thought Mac had been full of shit when he'd first told me that the MC was like a family, but they continuously proved it. Like now. I knew that Silk would prefer to stay and try to work out what the men were up to, but she knew my issues, knew what stress could do to me, so without a second thought, she was stepping up to help me out.

Hard to stay pissed off about my man needing to leave for a few days here and there for the club when that same club had brought this level of friendship and support to my life.

"Thanks, Silk, but I'm gonna try to wait till Mac finishes up."

Silk leaned over and ran her palm over my girl's hair.

"It's so hard when they're sick, even when you know it's nothing more than a new tooth. Like, the cuddles are great, but it's so hard not seeing them all full of life like they normally are."

"For sure."

Considering we normally had to basically crash tackle Cleo for a cuddle, I was enjoying her being so snuggly with me. But like Silk said, it was hard to see her so lethargic and unhappy.

Chapter 2

Mac

I didn't care if Cleo was only teething, baby girl was not happy and Zara was stressed out. That was a recipe for disaster and I was going to have to fucking leave them. Dammit. My woman was trying to hide it from me, probably in the hope of not getting me worried. Which was sweet, but I saw straight through it. As I hit Scout's office and pulled my phone out to call Blade, I decided I'd deal with Sabella as fast as I could and get back home. Sure, the fucker didn't deserve a quick death, but luckily for him, I rated my family over drawing out his end.

As I sat on the couch, the call connected.

"What's up, man?"

"Hey, Blade. Need to talk business. You able to speak freely?"

"Give me a sec."

I'd called him using the secure app Keys had created, but I had no clue where Blade was or who was around him that might overhear our conversation.

"Right. Talk to me."

"Sabella's pulled more shit and the Charons are done. I've got orders to come take care of him. You know where he's currently hiding?"

"Let me guess. This has something to do with that MC up in Boston, the Ice Riders?"

"Just got back from taking care of that little problem. That club doesn't exist anymore."

"Damn. What the fuck they'd do to earn a complete club wipe-out?"

"Fools came into our town and took a few of the old ladies hostage. Including my woman and the president's heavily pregnant wife. Held a fucking gun on her unborn baby. Sent her into early labor."

Not to mention Zara had a cataplexy attack and had injured herself because the fuckers wouldn't let anyone help her. But Zara didn't want the world knowing about her issues, and I understood and respected that.

"That'd do it. Okay, well, Sabella is certainly watching his back a little more than usual. But that's not all you need to consider. Don't suppose you've been online, seen a TV or had the radio on recently?"

"Been a little busy. Why?"

My mind raced with what might have happened big enough to hit mainstream media.

"California's on fire, my friend. Including a few in and around L.A. It's bad enough they've declared it a national disaster."

"Fuck. Is Sabella evacuating?"

"Nah, he's still in town, but he sent his wife and kids away last week. Fucker's been living it up with them gone. Since he got that fucking ledger and his hands on his money, he's been building up his human trafficking business. Including setting up a large stable of women and kids that he controls himself."

Blade's tone was ice cold, telling me exactly how he felt about things. My own fury ripped through me at his words. We should have fucking killed him instead of handing over that ledger of Silk's dad's to the bastard and letting him walk away. Giving him access to his money had hurt how many innocents? And we'd had the power to prevent it. Fuck.

"Not sure why you didn't tell me any of this sooner." I paused a moment but when he didn't give me an answer, I kept going. "We need to end his shit, and him. ASAP. I'll be heading into town with a crew of five soon. We'll be riding out first thing in the morning, so we'll get there Thursday. You got somewhere safe we can land?"

"About fucking time, man. I've been praying to hear those words outta your mouth for years. I don't have the power or the resources to take him out without starting a war, but together? We'll get this done. And, yeah, I got a place. It's nothing special but no one knows about it. It's not far from one of the fires, in Moreno Valley, but ignore the smoke. The fire's heading in the opposite direction so you and your men will be safe."

I'd have to be deaf to miss the obvious relief in his tone, and again I wondered why the hell he hadn't come to me sooner about this human trafficking shit. I'd wait till I saw him to ask the whys because I knew Blade well enough to know there had to be reason, and it would be one he wouldn't want to talk about over a phone. Or in person, for that matter. But I'd get to the bottom of it.

"Good deal. I need to go make arrangements with the club. We'll make our plan once we get there and you can talk us through everything you know. And, Blade? I mean *everything*. Until then, see if you can find out where his stable is. We need to free those women and kids. Gonna need somewhere for them to go, too."

A growl came over the line that had me jerking back in the seat. What the fuck?

"You don't think I've been trying to do just that? I can't find them. Trust me, if I'd been able to find the location, I'd have shut it down. Even if it was a suicide mission, I would have gone in."

"Well, after we grab Sabella, we'll be sure to ask some questions before we end his miserable life. See if you can set up someone to take care of any the victims we'll hopefully manage to round up from wherever the fuck he's got them stashed."

We ended the call and I went to find Scout and the others, more than ready to get this show on the road. Innocent lives were at risk, more every moment we waited.

I only allowed myself a quick glance at my girls as I plowed my way through the main room back toward the meeting room. I couldn't focus on them just yet. Not until

I vented some of this rage. I wished it wasn't so late, then I could head to the gym for a session, but that wasn't in the cards. Hopefully once I finished reporting to the others, they'd be able to bring me down a notch or two so I could go back to my girls with a semi-level head. It was pure insanity to ride out tonight. Arrow and I were tired from the flight back from New York, and Zara and Cleo needed me. Hell, I needed them tonight.

The others were quietly chatting when, after putting my phone back in a locker, I strode in.

"We're good to go tomorrow. The earlier, the fucking better. Got a place to land in the Moreno Valley. But there's wildfires all over the damn state so we need to watch ourselves."

Scout frowned as he watched me.

"What aren't you telling us?"

I shook my head. "I don't even know how to process this shit, prez. Just found out Sabella used the resources he got from that deposit box to set himself up in the flesh trade. Thanks to us, that fucker's been hurting innocents. Trading them like fucking furniture. He's got a fucking stable full of women and kids that he—" I couldn't even say it. "We shoulda just killed him when we had the chance."

Scout's face had turned grim as I'd spoken.

"Mac, you can't carry the guilt for his actions, brother. We did what we thought was best in the situation. If we'd taken him out, it would have brought war to our door. Lives would have been lost. It was a no-win situation and we did what we thought was best for all concerned. But, Mac? That's in the past, no one can turn back that clock. All we can do is go in and stop his shit now."

"We can't take him out clean. We need to question him to get details. My contact hasn't been able to find the location of his stable. But I asked him to find someone we can hand over the victims to once we rescue them."

Arrow spoke up. "The fires might actually work in our favor. Good for destroying evidence."

Scout stood up in a rush, clearly as affected as me, despite his calm words. "Right, so you boys will ride out first thing and head to this place you've got lined up. Maybe take a cage with you. And, Mac? I think at this point, you owe us the name of this contact of yours. We're putting a lot behind his intel."

I nodded, knowing this moment had been coming. "He goes by the name Blade. His real name is Jared Walker. I don't know exactly what happened to him, but he's always hated Sabella and only worked for him because Sabella's got something on him. Knowing what Sabella did to get me under his thumb, I can imagine what Blade was put through, but we've never spoken about it."

He nodded at me. "Thanks. Now go take your family home. I'll have Donna head over in the morning to stay with Zara. She and Keys will move into your spare room till you get back. That way they'll be close to help with Silk too, if she needs it."

With that, we were done and I led the others from the room, grabbing my shit out of the locker before going in search of my girls. I stopped short when I entered the main room. Silk was talking to Zara, who still sat with Cleo wrapped around her like a spider monkey. But she looked tired as hell. She was struggling and trying to hide it. Instantly forgetting everything but my girls, I strode over and gently took Cleo from her lap.

"C'mon, bunny, time to go home."

She gave me a nod and taking my outstretched hand, rose to her feet before releasing her hold on me.

"If you need to stay, I can take them."

I turned to Silk, who'd stood at the same time as Zara, concern for my wife clear on her face.

"Thanks, babe, but I've got it covered tonight." Especially since tonight could be our last together for a while. I didn't want to spend it upstairs in one of the rooms here.

Eagle and Taz appeared beside us.

"What do you need, brother?"

"Need to get my woman home—" That was when she dropped. "Fuck." Thankfully Silk was standing close enough to her so she could grab her and lower her back down onto the seat, since I had my arms full with Cleo. I hated when I couldn't be what both my wife and daughter needed me to be. I knew Zara always wanted me to put Cleo first, but fuck, it was hard to choose between them. I wanted to fix the world for both of them.

Silk was in my face a moment later, peeling a now crying Cleo from me so my arms were free to deal with Zara. I was torn. Clearly Cleo was not feeling well and wanted her mom or me, but Zara needed me too. It helped that I knew this attack would pass soon enough and Zara would be back with me, but I still needed to get her home.

"Want to take her upstairs? We'll get Cleo sorted and bring her up in a bit."

I shook my head as I scooped my woman up in my arms and held her against my chest.

"We're riding out in the morning for who knows how long. I want to get her home. You know how it is, she'll be fine in a little bit. Silk? Can you bring Cleo out to the car for me?"

"Sure, Mac. C'mon, little lady, let's get you buckled in so you can go home and help Daddy take care of Mommy."

I followed her out, staring at the tear-filled eyes of my little girl as she stared at her mom, with a hand reaching out for her. This shit gutted me every time, but it was part of life with Zara's medical issues. Normally Cleo rolled with it without much fuss, but she was a different kid when she was sick. Even if it was just her cutting a new tooth, as Zara suspected. I was grateful she was a pretty healthy kid, for the most part.

As I lowered Zara into the seat of the car and buckled her in, I couldn't help but resent the fact I had to leave her in the morning. Again. In this moment, I sure as fuck didn't want to, but I would. My club needed me to do this. Hell, those innocents Sabella was forcing to work on their backs needed me to do this. And I couldn't ignore the fact that until we neutralized Sabella, he would keep sending people after the club and our families. Might not end so well the next time someone pulled a fucking gun on Zara and Cleo. So, I would leave them in the morning to go make sure they were safe in the long run. No matter how much it fucking killed me to leave.

Zara

By the time Mac drove us home I'd recovered from the cataplexy attack. But my narcolepsy was still pulling me down, and I really wanted nothing more than to crawl into bed and sleep for a week. Well, part of me did. The other part wanted to get Cleo in bed, then get my sexy as hell husband naked to make the most of the night before he had to leave again in the morning.

While Mac got Cleo out of her car seat, I dragged myself out of my seat and toward the front door of our house. Unlocking things, I headed straight for the kitchen and got a bottle ready for Cleo, knowing Mac was getting her changed. I also pulled out the Baby Tylenol and got it ready to go too.

By the time Mac brought her out all changed and ready for bed, I had everything set.

"Babe, you look wrecked. Go on up to bed and I'll get Cleo settled."

Angry at myself because this was not how I planned to spend my night, I gave Cleo a kiss goodnight, then gave Mac a quick side hug before I headed upstairs and into our bedroom. I had no doubts Mac would get our girl medicated, fed and in her crib for the night without issue. I just hoped she'd stay there. She was normally a good sleeper, but with her out of sorts tonight, who knew how the night would go.

Kicking off my shoes, I sluggishly pulled the rest of my clothes off as my energy drained further with every movement I made. I was fumbling with the sheets when Mac's strong arms wrapped around my middle, before he leaned forward and pulled the bedding back. I ran my fingers up and down the new ink covering his forearm. Then, because I married a caveman, he picked me up and after pressing a kiss to my temple, laid me onto the mattress. I think I may have purred a little when, after he stripped and joined me in bed, he started stroking a hand through my hair.

"You heard me talk about tomorrow, yeah?"

While cataplexy stole my ability to control my muscles, I could still feel and hear everything that happened around me. I just couldn't respond, which drove me fucking nuts.

I nodded against the pillow, unable to keep my eyes open. "I did catch that. For how long this time?"

My voice came out harsher than I'd intended, but I was tired and on edge. And suddenly I wasn't feeling so great about the Charon MC stealing my man away from me again. I also really wanted to ask where he was going but I knew full well if I did ask, he wouldn't tell me because it was *club business*. There were times, like now, that I seriously regretted falling down this particular rabbit hole.

"I'm sorry, bunny. I wish I didn't have to go, but this trip will make sure that what happened at Marie's Cafe won't happen again. I'm the only one who can pull it off."

If he was the only one who could do it, then he was heading to southern California. Mac had been born and raised there before he'd left for the USMC.

"Gueshh you're heading wessst, then?"

Dammit, my words were starting to slur I was so tired. I wanted to have this discussion, but I didn't think my narcolepsy was going to let me.

"Yeah, I'll be heading to L.A. for a bit, but trust me, bunny, I'll be getting this shit done as fast as I can so I can get back to you and Cleo. I hate leaving you, especially when Cleo's not well. Scout's arranged for Keys and Donna to stay in the spare room. Donna's not working the day shift tomorrow so she can stay with you and help with Cleo."

I hummed and tried to nod again as that was all I could muster the energy for. A flash of anger lit me up that the club had just assumed I needed a damn babysitter. I'd learned how to successfully live with my conditions for the most part, and since having Cleo, things were a lot better, especially when I was around my sweet baby girl. Then just as quickly a wave of relief filled me at not having to be alone with my clingy and out-of-sorts daughter tomorrow. For all the club's faults, like the fact it was filled with overbearing cavemen, I couldn't knock how I could always count on them to back us up.

Mustering all my remaining energy, I turned into Mac's familiar body and wrapped my arm around him, snuggling in against him.

"Go to sleep, babe. I'll be waking you up later."

That made me smile as I drifted off. Mac had always been so damn insatiable, I had no doubt he'd be waking me up, probably more than once, before the sun rose in the morning.

Chapter 3

Zara

I stirred as wet heat engulfed my right nipple.

"Hmmm."

I lifted my hands to run my fingers over the smooth skin covering the hard muscles of Mac's biceps as he hovered over me. I blinked my eyes open to look up at him just as he released my breast to grin down at me.

"Morning, bunny."

"Uh huh."

Moving my hands to grip his face, I led him to my lips. He didn't need any more encouragement than that before he was kissing me slow and deep. Within moments, arousal buzzed through my body, making me restless for more. As I wriggled beneath him, he broke the kiss and chuckled as he pressed his forehead against mine.

"You hungry, babe?"

I jerked up and gave his lower lip a nip with my teeth. "You know I am, and you know exactly what I need to ease it, so quit teasing me."

"Oh, but teasing you is so much fun. But I'm feeling rather hungry myself."

My breath sped up as he moved down my body, his gaze never leaving mine as he kissed a path along the way, running his tongue down a stretch mark over my tummy before finally getting to his intended destination.

A sigh slipped free as he wrapped a palm around each of my thighs and pushed them wide to give himself enough room to lower down. My heart thundered in my chest as his hot breath washed over my flesh. Then he finally quit teasing and stroked his tongue up through my folds before he wrapped his lips around my clit to suck and torment the sensitive little nub.

Within seconds, I was moaning and trying to wriggle away from the intensity of the sensations he was pulling from me. He growled and shifted a hand to my lay over my tummy, keeping me pinned down. He put the other hand to good use a moment later by sliding two fingers inside me and going straight for my g-spot as he wrapped his mouth around my clit again.

I tried to hold off, to make the pleasure last longer, but I didn't stand a chance. My climax burst over me within moments. My body arched as I whisper-yelled his name. My body went limp with cataplexy, as it did with just about every orgasm Mac gave me, and he moved to press kisses over my thighs and stomach as he stroked his fingers within my core, gently bringing me down from my high.

As soon as I was able, I ran a palm over his head, the soft stubble he shaved from his skull each morning brushing against my skin as I lovingly caressed the only part of Mac I could currently reach.

"Need to be inside you, Zara. I missed you so fucking much."

"You were only gone one night, babe. But yeah, I missed you too. Feels strange to sleep without you here beside me."

He scooped me up in his arms as he sat back on the mattress. I wrapped my arms around his neck and my legs loosely around his hips as he reached down and lined up the head of his cock with my pussy. His other hand was on my ass and I tightened my legs on him as he pulled my body down over his erection. I threw my head back as he stretched my core open, his length throbbing within me.

"Hmm, so good."

He shifted his grip to my hips and guided me up and down his length. His nose ran up against mine, and with a groan, I moved my hands to cup his jaw.

"I love you, Jacob."

He stilled for a moment as a wide grin spread over his face. I was the only one who ever called him by his legal name, and I didn't do it often.

"Love you too, Claire."

Yeah, he was definitely the only who used my real first name. Zara was my middle name, but it was the only name most people knew me by.

I tightened my grip, tilting his face so I could take control over our kiss as his hands on my body controlled our lovemaking. As our tongues danced, his thick erection slid in and out of my core, Mac making sure he ground against my clit each time he bottomed out. My body was humming with arousal, sensitizing my skin and sending my thoughts into a happy jumble of chaos.

Panting, I broke the kiss and shifted my legs so I was now kneeling over Mac. He smirked at me when I pushed his shoulders, trying to get him to lie back. He resisted for a minute, until I growled at him, then with another husky chuckle, he laid back across the mattress.

"Fuck, bunny, you look like a goddess leaning over me like this. C'mon, babe, ride me like you mean it."

I took him slow and deep, enjoying my short time of being in control of my big, bad, biker. I knew he wouldn't give me long. It just wasn't in his nature to let me lead. He needed to be in control. It was wired into his DNA and I loved it. I also loved battling him for control once in a while, reminding him that he didn't marry a pushover.

His hands reached up and cupped my breasts, rubbing his callused thumbs over the tips until I was shuddering over him and panting through the arousal.

I sped up my movements, swiveling my hips in the way I knew would drive him wild, while I reached behind me to run my nails lightly over his balls and he growled out a curse.

"Fuck."

Then my world spun and I was on my back with his big, sexy body covering mine.

"Play time is over, bunny."

I grinned at his growled words before he took my mouth in a hard kiss as he reentered me with a powerful thrust of his hips that stole my breath.

I moved my hips with him on every stroke, chasing my climax as Mac's inner beast took control and he pounded into me like his life depended on fucking me as hard as he could. I fucking loved when he lost control like this. Nothing made me feel more loved than the time he couldn't bare another moment of taking it slow. He wanted me so much, he had to have me that instant. And all the growly alpha male bullshit he sprouted off didn't hurt a girl's ego, either.

"C'mon, bunny. Give it to me. You're mine, all fucking mine and I want your orgasm right this fucking second. You hear me?"

As though my body was waiting for him to give his permission, my world blew apart. I dug my nails into his shoulders as my vision darkened and filled with stars as I shattered into a million pieces. Then his face was pressed in against my neck, his shout of completion muffled against my skin as he filled my womb with his seed.

Damn, but I loved my man.

33

Mac

After a mind-blowing round of sex with my woman, I'd cleaned her up and had let her snuggle back down to sleep. It'd been the very early hours of the morning when I'd first woken her. That had been a couple of hours ago, so I figured I'd be safe to wake her again real soon for another round. Or two. Needed to get all the loving in I could before I had to leave her.

Propping myself up on my elbow I looked down at her. She was curled on her side, facing away from me, her strawberry blond hair a sexy mess over the pillow as she peacefully slept. The sheet had crept down, revealing her from the waist up and the early morning light highlighted the silvery lines that marred the perfection of her back. Every time I saw those scars, fury and pain sliced me deep to my soul.

A rival club had taken her from me and we'd only just gotten to her in time to save her. Sledge, the previous president of the Iron Hammers MC, had been on the verge of thrusting his cock inside my woman when Taz put a bullet in his brain. But even though we got to her in time to save her from being raped, we hadn't been in time to save her from being strung up and whipped raw down her back, all the way from her shoulders to her thighs. Thankfully, only a few of the cuts had scarred. But it didn't change the fact I wished it had never happened, that I'd found her sooner. It also reminded me again why I had to leave her in a few hours. No way was I going to stand by and allow Sabella to force his shit on any other victims, or to send more assholes after my club, my family.

Needing to wipe all those thoughts away to stay sane, I moved to spoon up behind my girl. With a completely fucking adorable tiny whimper, she wriggled her ass back against me, making my already hard cock throb for her. Moving her hair out of the way, I pressed a trail of soft kisses across her shoulder. Then, at the same time as I buried my face in against her neck, I lifted her leg over mine, pulled my hips back then slid my dick into her welcoming heat.

I kept my movements slow and smooth, waking her up from the inside gently.

"Hmmm."

She arched against me, clenching down on my cock as she reached a hand back to hold my head against her. Not that she needed to. I wasn't going anywhere any time soon. Running my fingers up her thigh, I skipped over her pussy and headed up to her tits. She'd stopped breastfeeding Cleo about a month back, but her nipples were still more sensitive than they'd been before she'd gotten pregnant, not to mention her tits were bigger now, too. I fucking loved the extra lushness to her curves. I slipped my other arm under her neck so I could use that hand to play with her tits too. Wrapping both palms around her mounds, I used my hold to pull her down onto my cock as I started to thrust a little faster and harder into her.

It didn't take long for her to start whimpering as she tried to wriggle away from an orgasm that was no doubt rapidly building inside of her. I moved one hand down to wrap around her waist to hold her back against me as I continued to thrust into her.

"Stop trying to run away, bunny. You're mine and I got you. You gonna blow apart for me again? Come all over my cock."

She shuddered against me.

"Fucking dirty talker. You know I'm close, quit talking and fuck me already."

With a chuckle, I pinched her nipple at the same time as I flicked her clit and thrust in deep. That was enough to set her off. When she rolled onto her front to bury her face into the pillow as she screamed her release, I followed her over and propped myself up on my arms as I started pounding into her from behind, chasing my own climax. It didn't take long to lose myself in her warm heat that was still rippling against my flesh from her orgasm. With a groan, I filled her up again, cursing that she was on birth control so my seed wouldn't take. I'd fucking loved seeing her grow round with my daughter, couldn't wait to do it again. But Zara wasn't ready. She told me she needed at least a few years to deal with raising our little spitfire Cleo Beatrice before she'd be willing to do it all again.

As much as I didn't want to wait, I did understand her point. Our little Cleo was going to keep us on our toes for the rest of our lives.

While Zara was down with her cataplexy, I kissed my way over the scars on her back, stroking my palms over her skin, across her ribs and down over her sexy ass.

"Love you, Zara, so fucking much. I hate that I gotta leave you so soon but I have to make sure nothing ever hurts you again. I can't even bear the thought of it."

Chapter 4

Mac

Half an hour after kissing my girls goodbye and leaving them safely tucked away in our house, I was standing out in the fucking cold of the early morning at the clubhouse, prepping to ride to California.

Scout was there to see us off and make sure we had everything he thought we might need. We were leaving our cuts in our saddle bags and riding without colors. Bank and Jazz were bringing one of the vans, just in case, while Eagle, Arrow and I were taking our bikes. I'd just come outside from taking a leak when Scout came over to stand close enough to me to talk without being overheard.

"I wasn't pulling your chain about you being rewarded after this is done. You're lead on this, just like up in New York, then when you get back we're gonna have a sit down and discuss some things."

I frowned over at him.

"Don't play fucking games, prez. I need my head clear for this, not worried about what's gonna blow up when I get back."

He shook his head with a chuckle. "That, right there, is why you're fucking perfect. Even though you know as I'm your president, you should just do what I tell you, you're not afraid to ask questions." He sighed and glanced around at the others, making sure we were still out of earshot. "All I'll say is there's gonna be more than one new patch handed out in the near future, yeah?"

My frowned deepened. "Yeah, thanks, prez. Clear as fucking mud there. Okay, look, the sooner we get going, the sooner we can come back and you can finally make some fucking sense."

He barked out a laugh and clapped me on the back before whistling to get everyone's attention.

"Ride safe, brothers, and keep me posted. I want at least daily check-ins, Mac."

We all nodded as we put our helmets on and saddled up, ready to ride. The roar of the three beasts filled the air as we rolled out ahead of the van and made our way out of town. My heart was heavy as we put Bridgewater in our mirrors. Missed my girls already. As we took off down the highway in the light of the rising sun, I sent up a prayer that Cleo was only cutting a new tooth and it would come through fast so she could be a happy girl for Zara while I was gone.

As we crossed the country, we only stopped when we absolutely had to. All of us wanted this run to be done with and in the past. We stopped to catch a few hours of sleep in Las Cruces in New Mexico before we kept going through to Moreno Valley. Blade hadn't been kidding about the smoke from all the fires. The closer we got, the more eerie it was. By the time we'd finally arrived at the trailer Blade told me about, we'd put scarves over our faces to be able to breathe thought all the smoke. Blade's place looked like it was a stiff wind away from falling down. The three of us backed up in a line across the front yard and Bank pulled the van up beside us on the road's edge.

Bank came up to me. "Damn, this smoke is bad. You sure we're safe here?"

I shrugged, feeling a little on edge myself at all the smoke. "Blade said the fire was heading away from here."

I strode up to the door and before I could bang on the thing, it opened and revealed the man who'd once been the only man I'd trusted at my back.

"Blade, man, good to see you."

"Same goes, Mac."

We did that manly back-slap hug thing quickly before I pulled back to introduce everyone.

"Blade, these are a few of my Charon brothers—Eagle, Arrow, Bank and Jazz."

Blade's gaze took them all in. I knew from experience he was gauging the threat level of each man in mere moments. My club brothers gave him the same once-over, even Jazz. Kid had guts. Always made me nervous to bring an unknown on a mission, and that's what a prospect was. Although, Jazz had been prospecting for well over a year now, so he really should be a patched in brother by this point. I'd never personally seen the kid in a fight, though, or handle a gun, so I was still cautious of having him at my six. But he was a Charon, so I did trust him to do his part. I knew Scout wouldn't have sent him otherwise.

"Good to meet you all. Come on in and let's get this party started. Can't tell you how long I've been waiting for this day."

Blade hadn't changed much over the years. Still had his short beard neatly trimmed, and the facial hair still did nothing to hide the sharp cut of his jaw. His steel-blue eyes were as ice-cold as always. The dark dress pants and buttoned up white shirt were the same too. Although, some of the ink his rolled up sleeves revealed hadn't been there last time I'd seen him. But considering I'd filled in one of my arms down to the wrist since then myself, I wasn't about to get on his case for not telling me about his new ink. He definitely still looked like the made man he'd been forced to become. Maybe once we got Sabella in the ground where the fucker belonged, Blade could break free and find a life for himself.

We all filed inside the trailer and instantly I could see an issue.

"I doubt we're going to get this handled in one day—"

Blade held up his hand to stop me. "Let me stop you there. I don't sleep here normally. There's plenty of room for you all, assuming one of you doesn't mind taking the couch."

"That'll work. Why don't you sleep here?"

Arrow didn't bother to hide the suspicion in his voice, which I could understand. I wasn't sure what to make of the situation as it stood, either.

"This is my hidden place. No one in Sabella's crew knows about it. The only way to keep it that way is to not spend nights here. As Mac knows, Sabella encourages us to rat each other out. If I was regularly sleeping out here, he'd know about it sooner or later and I need this place off his radar."

Arrow raised his brow at me and I looked away. "Story for another day, brother."

I'd never told the club about my history. They knew I had ties to some folks here in L.A., but not how those ties came to be. Scout knew a little more after what went down with Silk, then with Zara, but even then I kept it to the bare minimum.

"Blade? Where's the info you got for us? We need to get a plan in place ASAP to get this shit dealt with."

Zara

With a sigh, I ran my gaze over my fussy baby, who was currently crying and pulling her ear as she laid in her crib. In the two days since Mac left, she's only gotten worse.

"Ah, baby girl, I don't think it's a new tooth at all."

I leaned down and scooped her up in my arms and she instantly clung to me, rubbing her face against my shoulder.

"How about we take her into the doctor this morning? I'm thinking it might be an ear infection with the way she's tugging on that ear of hers."

With another sigh, I nodded to Donna. "Yeah, I was just thinking the same thing. She's been so healthy, it kills me when she's sick."

Donna came over and gave my shoulder a squeeze. "Means you're a good mom if you feel it that deep. Don't worry, every kid gets them and they're easy to treat. Want me to call through to Dr. Stevenson while you get her changed?"

"Thanks, that'd be great."

Since Donna worked at the hospital that also housed the doctors' clinic, she knew who I needed to see without having to ask, which I was grateful for. I'd struggled to sleep deeply without Mac beside me. Add in worrying about Cleo being ill, and it's been even harder for me to get enough rest.

Knowing I wouldn't have long to wait, I set about getting my grumpy girl dressed and ready for the day while trying not to stress too much about what could be wrong with her. My mom-brain came up with all sorts of options, other than the obvious ear infection as I picked up and dressed my daughter. Donna helped me get a little food into her then we were off to the doctor.

"If I haven't said this yet, thank you so much for you and Keys coming over while Mac's away."

"Oh, honey, you don't need to thank us. We're family, this is what we do. We look after each other. I'm just sorry I can't stay with you today."

I waved her off. "You have to work. Like you said, Cleo's probably just got an ear infection. Doc will give me a prescription, and she'll be back to full throttle in no time, I'm sure."

Donna smirked with a nod. "Damn straight. Nothing will ever keep that little spitfire of yours down for long."

I turned around to look at my poor little munchkin, who was looking utterly miserable in her car seat. It sure was strange to see her so quiet.

A few minutes later, we pulled into the clinic's parking lot and I didn't bother even getting her stroller out. I knew Cleo wasn't going to let go of me while she was feeling so unwell. Once again, I was so damn grateful to have Donna with me, who dealt with locking the car and grabbing the diaper bag. At ten months old, Cleo was heavy to hold for any length of time, especially if she was sick and basically a dead weight in my arms like she was today.

After only waiting ten minutes in the waiting room, Dr. Stevenson called us through and after doing a fast examination of one very cranky Cleo, confirmed her ear was indeed infected. The internal part of me that was running every worst case scenario it could come up with finally started to relax.

"Cleo's not allergic to anything, is she?"

"Haven't found anything yet. Although, this will be her first time needing anything stronger than Baby Tylenol."

"Okay. Well, I'll prescribe some amoxicillin for her, and just keep an eye on her for a couple hours after the first dose for any reaction."

And that quickly my mom radar was back up and running.

"What kind of reaction?"

"If, and it's a big if, she does have an adverse reaction, it'll most likely be a rash, or she might start having trouble breathing."

"Maybe we should try something else?"

"Zara, the chances are low that she'll react to it, and anything else I prescribe has the same possible allergy risks. You'll be fine. Just watch her closely for a few hours after the first dose, and if you notice a rash, bring her in, or if she's having trouble breathing, call for an ambulance, okay?"

I took a few deep breaths trying to relax while the doc tapped away at her computer, sorting out the prescription. Donna leaned in and gave my arm a squeeze before she gently stroked Cleo's hair.

"Try to relax, Zara. This is all totally normal and at some point, every kid gets an ear infection or two. We'll get this handled in no time."

A few minutes later, we were out of the clinic and Donna was wincing while looking at her watch.

"I've gotta go start my shift. Are you all right to drive to the pharmacy and back home? I can get Keys to—"

I waved her off. "I can drive, Donna. Thank you for all your help this morning. It's been huge, but I'm sure I can handle things for a few hours on my own."

When I was stressed, I got cranky. And Donna asking if I could drive me and my daughter home pushed me close to the edge. I was trying to not get angry with her, but dammit, I wasn't a fucking child. Yeah, I had some medical conditions. Conditions I'd lived with for years on my own. Before Mac I was completely alone and I survived just fine. I appreciated my friends wanting to help, but there were moments where it got suffocating and had me wanting to lash out.

The look on Donna's face said I'd hurt her with my words, but I knew if I said anything else I'd only make it worse. My emotions were all over the damn place this week. Especially when it came to the club. So before I said anything else I'd no doubt regret later, I turned and nearly ran to my car. As I strapped Cleo into her seat, I cursed silently that I didn't ask if Donna had a way to get home after her shift. Hopefully Keys was free to come get her because once I got the medicine for Cleo, I wasn't leaving the house again. And I kind of wished they weren't staying with me now. I was also a little glad that Mac wasn't here to see my losing my shit so badly over the fact everyone was being way too helpful and our girl was sick.

Chapter 5

Mac

We'd stayed up late the previous night, going over Blade's information and tossing around ideas before we'd called it a night. Then, this morning, after we'd all gotten a few hours' sleep, we got back to it until we had a plan formed. It was around noon when we finally got something solidly mapped out enough I felt comfortable reporting back to Scout.

The way he told me I'd be rewarded for all my work, combined with the way Arrow was watching me like a hawk, had me wondering what the fuck was going on. It also had me being a lot more careful of my every move and what I reported back to my president.

Using the secure app Keys created for us, I dialed Scout's number as I sat back on Blade's couch.

"Whatcha got for me?"

"Got a plan sorted out. Going to set it in motion as soon as you give the okay."

"I like the speed you're getting this shit done, brother. What's the plan?"

"Basically, we're gonna bait a trap and catch him that way. Blade knows of a secluded cabin that's near the fires so it'll be empty and no one will be around. The fires are predicted to cut in near it but not over it, so we'll be safe enough but free to light the place up afterward to cover our tracks. We're going to tell Sabella we have a couple girls for his stable that he won't be able to resist. See if he bites. If he doesn't initially bite, we'll have to find some photos to use to prove we have what we're trying to sell him. But Blade thinks if we play it right, saying we're in a rush to move them because of the fires, he'll jump without too much proof. He'll no doubt bring extra security with him, but we can handle that."

"And once you have the fucker?"

"We'll get all the information we can about his human trafficking shit out of him, then take him out. We'll stage it to look like he and his lackeys were trying to leave the cabin when the fire caught up with them."

We just needed to make sure we didn't kill with bullets or damage any bones when we used knives. We'd add accelerant to the scene to make sure they were nothing but charred bones by the time anyone finds them.

"Did Blade find someone who can take care of the women and kids?"

"Yeah, he's found a cop off Sabella's books and a shelter that'll take them in."

"Good work. Plan sounds solid, keep me posted as you go."

We finished up the call and I stood to go find Blade, who was in the kitchen.

"We're good to go. Put the message through to Sabella and let's see if he bites."

When Blade pulled out his phone, I grabbed his wrist. "Whoa. I figured you'd use a burner phone for this one."

His cold gaze caught mine and stayed locked there. "He won't know who it is if I use a burner. He'll never go for it quickly. If it's from me, he'll trust the source and, hopefully, come running."

"It also leaves a trail back to you."

He shrugged. "Once Sabella is in the ground, I'm done here, anyhow. And who's going to be left to figure it out? He'll bring his most trusted with him and we'll take them all out. The rest of his men have scattered with the fire evacuations, so it's going to take a long time before anyone even thinks of looking at phone records. By then, I plan to be long gone."

I opened my mouth to ask him what his plans were for afterward when he lifted his chin and pulled free from my grip on his wrist, letting me know he had no intention of continuing the conversation.

He typed into his phone for a few minutes before he slipped it back in his pocket. "It's done. Let's load up and get over there. I haven't given him the address yet, so we've got time to get the place rigged up."

It didn't take long to round up everyone, then deciding to leave the bikes behind, we all piled into the van. We then headed over to the small cabin that was all but lost in among all the trees and shrubbery. Blade was right, it was perfect for what we were hopefully going to do here. The thick smoke in the air wasn't ideal, but we had Jazz permanently on his electronic devices, monitoring the relevant websites for warnings and information on the fire's progress.

When Blade got the message that Sabella was interested, it didn't take long to pass on the location and to hear that he was on his way to view the packages. Excitement filled the air as we rushed to finish getting ready. Arrow set himself up a tree with a sniper rifle loaded with tranq darts. Eagle had the same weapon and hid himself up on the roof of the cabin. They both had scarves tied around their faces to help them breathe though this god-awful smoke. It really gave this whole situation a post-apocalyptic feel I didn't like one bit.

I headed back inside the cabin with Bank and Blade. Jazz was sitting at the rear of the cabin with his phone and an Ipad on the table in front of him.

"Status on the fire?"

"If the wind stays as it is, we should be safe here. I'll let you know the minute that changes. If it changes."

"Good man."

Then we waited. I'd checked my gun and knives several times by the time we heard an engine cut off outside the cabin.

"Game on, men."

Jazz kept watching the screens, but pulled his gun free and held it on the table, pointed at the door, his finger against the barrel ready to slide down to the trigger if needed. I stood to the side of the door, ready to take out whoever came in and Bank followed Blade out, with his weapon out and ready. Unlike the rifles, we didn't have tranqs for our handguns so if we shot, we needed to be damn careful where we hit them, but if it came down to their lives or ours, we'd deal with the bullets later.

"Who is your friend, Blade?"

Sabella's voice sounded exactly the same. Mac was certain his natural accent wasn't as heavy as he made it sound.

"Just someone who found himself with a couple of packages he needed to move quickly."

I heard Sabella's growl from where I stood, a sure sign he was not happy about dealing with someone new. He was about to be a hell of a lot less happy once we got him inside.

"He goes by the name Bank, but he doesn't talk much. You want to come and inspect the products, or what? That fire's way too fucking close for my liking."

Having the fire so near doubled in our favor at this moment. Not only would it help us get rid of evidence, it also gave us the perfect reason to be in a rush and for Blade to be more nervous than usual.

"This is not how we normally conduct such business, but yes, these fires are forcing all our hands on things of late. Take me to see them."

"Follow Bank and we'll get this shit sorted."

Bank would hate having Sabella and his men at his back. I knew I would, but we had him covered. He strode through the door, followed by Sabella. Then over the next few seconds, our plan went like clockwork. I grabbed Sabella's arm, spinning him face-first against the wall with his arm up behind his back and his face pressed against the rough timber of the cabin's wall. Before he knew what was going on, I had the muzzle of my gun pressed to his side, below the ribs. Not an instant kill shot, but it'd fucking hurt and prevent him getting away if he tried anything.

While I was handling Sabella, Eagle and Arrow had darted his men as they'd attempted to follow him inside. I glanced over to see Blade slice the throats of the men before he moved to pull the darts free and pocket the evidence.

"What the fuck is going on?"

Yep, that accent wasn't sounding very Italian at all now that the chips were down and he knew his life was at stake.

"You fucked with the wrong club, Sabella. The Charon MC always looks after its own, always rights the wrongs done against them and those they care about."

I took some pleasure in the shudder that ran through his body. Before he could say another word, Blade strode over and took his arm from my control. I stood back with my weapon trained on him.

"I wouldn't recommend fighting Blade as we get you settled. That fire isn't giving us the time to knock you out and wait for you to wake back up, but if you force our hand, we will. And if we have to knock you out, we'll be taking you back to Texas. Scout's more than a little pissed over the fact your bullshit sent his wife into early labor. Just imagine what he'd do to you with no time limitations on him?"

Watching this fucker who'd ruined so many lives sweat and stumble as Blade dragged him across to the center of the room before he tied him to a chair we'd put there for him, had me grinning. It was time for some long overdue justice to be served. Charon style.

Zara

By the time I'd made it to the pharmacy and then home with my super clingy Cleo, I rather regretted my flash of anger that would probably mean Keys and Donna wouldn't be staying here tonight. I'd definitely changed my mind on the brief thought I had about how I was glad Mac wasn't here to see me lose my shit. I wanted him here. I wanted him to be holding me as I measured out this pink liquid and gave it to our daughter. I didn't care if he saw me lose my shit. I mean, it wasn't like he hadn't seen it happen before.

It wasn't that unusual for me to get so angry at my illnesses and all they stopped me from doing that I'd start ranting about it. I'd even thrown a mug across the room once. It had shattered against the wall and made a hell of a mess. Mac had calmly taken me upstairs to thoroughly distract me, then he'd cleaned the kitchen up while I'd slept.

Although, since having Cleo, I'd noticed I didn't go down with cataplexy attacks as easily as I used to, at least not in situations that involved Cleo. Guess my maternal instinct overrode the disorder when it came to looking after my baby girl.

Not opening my eyes, I rubbed my palm up and down Cleo's back, who was now fast asleep on my chest as I relaxed back against the couch. I wanted to call Mac so badly, but didn't want to risk catching him at a bad time. The last thing I needed was him getting shot or hurt because I distracted him with a phone call for no reason, other than I was simply missing him. Cleo made a little whimpering noise and I opened my eyes to check her over. The moment my gaze focused on her, my heart stopped in my chest. A bright red rash had formed across her cheek and down her neck.

"No, no, no."

I gently shifted her so I could stand and then I was off. Clutching her against me, I rushed from the back of the house and through the yard, over to Taz and Flick's place. Along with Silk and Eagle, our houses were all next to each other and the men had taken out the fences so our yards were now one big area. It made it so it only took me seconds to get to the back of their place.

I started yelling the moment I was through their rear door.

"Taz? Flick? I need help!"

Taz came running first, little Lolly in his big, beefy arms as he pounded down the hallway toward me.

"What's wrong? What do you need?"

"I need you to take me to the hospital. Cleo's reacting to the medicine I just gave her."

Flick had joined us by the time I'd finished speaking, and she took Lolly from Taz. "Take Zara's car, I'll follow you."

As we raced back toward my house, Cleo stared to rasp her breaths in and out. I looked down to see her little lips had swollen up and my heart lurched. Dr. Stevenson said to call an ambulance, but that would take just as long, if not longer, than us going to the hospital so I kept moving. *Please let us get to the hospital in time.*

"It's getting worse, Taz."

"Fuck. Where're your keys?"

I nodded to the kitchen counter and he snatched them up before sprinting for the front door with me hot on his heels. As Taz got behind the wheel, I got in the front passenger seat, keeping Cleo in my arms.

"Hurry, Taz. She's struggling to breathe."

"Call the hospital and let 'em know we're on our way."

I nodded and pulled my phone from my pocket. The second the call connected I spoke.

"My baby's got this horrible rash and now she's not breathing right. We're on our way into the hospital now. About five minutes out."

"Come straight to the emergency entrance when you get here and we'll have doctors standing by to take care of her. Do you know what your child is reacting to, ma'am?"

"I've just given her amoxicillin for an ear infection. Dr. Stevenson told me to watch for reactions."

"What are your and your child's names, ma'am?"

"Zara Miller and my baby is Cleo Miller. We're nearly there now."

"That's good. I'm going to go and get everything ready for your arrival. Deep breaths and we'll be here ready to help you both through this."

I hung up the phone and stared at the screen for a moment.

"I should call Mac."

But what had I said? He couldn't do anything from where he was. It would just stress him out, especially when I didn't know what they were going to do for Cleo yet.

"Not sure that's a good idea, luv. They were doing something big today. I'll let Scout know as soon as I can, and when Mac next checks in, Scout will pass the message on to call you. That's the best we can do."

His voice was tight and a wave of sympathy for him rolled through me. The three of them, Mac, Taz and Eagle, had always had each other's backs while they served in the USMC and then afterward in the club. It must be killing Taz to have been left behind on this one.

At the same time, I also felt a jolt of anger that the club had my man so far away from me and Cleo when we needed him so desperately here. Not for the first time, I wondered what the fuck could be so important he had to leave for the second time in a week.

"Hate this."

"I know, luv. But we're family and we've got you covered. Just lean on us and let us help you."

I wasn't sure if he'd said that for my benefit or to remind himself, but we reached the hospital before I could ask anything else.

Taz pulled up right outside the door and there was a team waiting for us. A nurse opened my door and I stood, passing Cleo over to him. He turned and put my poor little girl on the gurney they'd brought out for her and the entire team rushed inside the hospital.

In that moment, my adrenaline ran out and I was spent. My need to see Cleo safe had prevented my body from doing what it normally did in intense situations, but now that Cleo was getting medical care, I was left standing there reeling. In a fast rush, I felt my cataplexy roll through me and there was nothing I could do to prevent myself collapsing to the ground.

"Fuck! Zara!"

Taz had gotten out of the car thankfully and was able to catch me before I hit the ground. Then I was up in his arms as he carried me inside the hospital.

"I've got you, luv. We're just going to sit here 'till you come back."

Every time I got furious with the club for something, like taking my man away from me when I need him so much, someone else the club brought into my life, like Taz, stepped up and did something so fucking beautiful and kind, that I couldn't possibly stay mad with the Charon MC.

Chapter 6

Mac

With my arms crossed, I stood perfectly still as I watched Sabella strain against the restraints that held him firmly to the chair.

"So unfortunate that we don't have endless time."

My words had the intended effect and got his full attention. I grinned at the fiery glare he aimed my way.

"You know you won't get away with this. My men will come for your little pissant club and take every one of you out. Your women and children will be sold off—"

Blade's fist connecting with his jaw cut his words off, thankfully. Blade didn't say a word, just silently slipped back into the shadows behind Sabella once his shot was delivered. Shaking myself back to the plan, I cleared my throat.

"Normally Scout delivers this little speech but since he's not here, I guess I get to do it. I hope I get it right. Wouldn't want my president disappointed in me…"

Arrow snorted from his place at the door. Once Sabella and his men were all taken down, Arrow had climbed down from his perch and he now stood guard at the door, keeping watch on the driveway and surrounding trees while Eagle stayed on the roof, looking out from there.

"Know much about Greek mythology, Antonio?"

"What the fuck does that have to do with anything?"

"In Greek mythology, the Charon was the ferryman. It was up to the Charon to decide if a soul would pass to the Elysian Fields or Hades. That's who our club is named after. The Greek ferryman who decides the fate of those presented before him for judgment." I paused for a moment before I pulled my knife free and stepped closer to him. "You messed with the wrong club, Antonio. You would have been better off to not gain our attention, but now that you have, we're going to fucking deal with you once and for all. Because no one fucks with us and walks away."

I made fast work of slicing his jacket and shirt from him. I couldn't help the growl that rose from my throat at the scratch marks on his arms. I ran the tip of my blade down one, slicing open his skin.

"Where are you keeping them?"

He hissed through the pain of the slice before answering me. "Who?"

"You know *exactly* who. The innocent women and children you abuse and charge others to use. Where are you keeping them?"

A spark of humor in his gaze had me clenching my jaw.

"Your intention is to kill me regardless of what I say, no? Why would I tell you a thing?"

"Because the how is still up for negotiation. I learned all sorts of fun things in the USMC, in addition to what you taught me."

The humor died and I saw a flash of fear before he locked it down and raised his chin.

"You don't have the time to break me."

I called over my shoulder to Jazz. "We still good with the fires?"

"Yep, we're good. Plenty of time."

Well, that was a lie. We didn't have a heap of time, but I appreciated him adding that for Sabella's benefit.

"Think I'll start with a classic. Feel free to start talking at any time. You start giving me the details I want, I'll stop." I snatched the pliers from my back pocket and clamped it onto the nail on his right index finger as I wrapped my left hand over his, holding it down for what I was about to do. "Still got nothing to say?"

He clenched his jaw and glared hard at me. Without taking my gaze from his, I tore the first of his nails free. A small grunt of pain was all the stoic bastard allowed himself. So I moved onto the next nail.

When I ran out of fingernails, I stood back to take him in. He was red in the face and sweating, but nowhere near breaking. I was a little impressed. I'd figured he would have gotten soft over the years of being the big boss and no longer having to do dirty work himself.

"The longer you hold out on us, the worse you make this for yourself. You won't win this one. And if the fire does get too close, we'll just load you up and take you with us. Then we'll have endless time."

His Adam's apple bobbed as he swallowed.

"I will tell you nothing. And you can live with the fact that there was nothing you could do to save any of them. All those sweet innocents forced to spread their legs and open their mouths on command. Without me to say when they've had enough they'll be used even more harshly, until their bodies give out."

A low growl filled the room before Blade stepped forward and, with a grip on Sabella's hair, he ripped the man's head back so hard I was worried he might snap his spine.

"Easy, man. We still need him alive."

The stupid fucker grinned at Blade. "I still have her, you know. I couldn't bring myself to sell such a rare beauty. Even after all this time, your—"

Blade released his hold and backhanded him across the face.

"You lying bastard. You don't say her name. You have no fucking right to even breathe in her direction!"

He spat out a mouthful of blood. "I wondered if this was you trying something, so I gave instructions. You see, all this time she's been my toy, my favorite. But today she's getting to be everyone's favorite. My men are doing all sorts of nasty things to her and won't stop until I tell them to. And they've wanted a taste of her for a long time. What do you think they're doing to her right now, Blade?"

I'd figured this situation was personal for Blade, but this was a whole heap of new information.

"Blade, step back. Now. You kill him, we'll never find her. Go out to the van and get the battery. We *will* break him."

The situation took on a new level of urgency. He might deserve to have his death drawn out, but getting to those women and kids as quickly as possible was more important. Especially the one he just mentioned. Images of my sister flashed across my vision as I breathed through the pain those memories always brought on.

Blade wasn't the only one who needed to calm down before we killed him too fast.

I kneeled to remove his shoes, socks, then cut off his pants until he sat naked before us.

Blade returned with the box I'd packed for today and set it on the table. I went to it and started pulling what I needed out of the box.

"Anything you want to tell me?"

Rage was vibrating off him. "I had no idea he still had her. He told me she'd died."

As I wired things up, ready to start this next step in breaking down Sabella, I kept my voice low so hopefully only Blade would hear me.

"When we get the information, you can't take off on us. It'll be suicide for you to run in there on your own and you know it. We've got your back on this."

"I need to get to her."

"I know. Trust me, I get it. My sister, she was—" I still struggled to say it. "I get it, okay? But if you go storming in there all Lone Ranger, those men will kill them all and you. We need to do this controlled so at the end of the day, they're the ones in the ground and we're not. Understood?"

He was still strung tight and I could see in his gaze the warring emotions causing chaos in his mind. But he gave me a nod.

"Right. Now let's make this fucker pay."

Zara

It was hours later before I found myself alone beside my little girl who was now peacefully sleeping in a hospital bed. We were still in the ER, with noise and people moving around us but that was easy to block out as I focused on the rise and fall of Cleo's torso as she breathed.

The swelling around her lips and face had gone down since the doctor had given her whatever the fuck they did to stop her reaction. The rash over her arms didn't look so nasty either. I was still scared to take my eyes off her for even a second, but it helped that the doctor and nurses were all certain she was heading for a full recovery.

It seemed so insane that something as simple as a damn ear infection nearly cost my baby her life. Stupid fucking drugs. They helped so much. Hell, without my medications I'd barely be able to function, I'd be so tired all the time. But when shit like this happened, I hated them. Especially when I was the one who'd given Cleo the medicine that nearly took her from me. My mother's guilt was pulling at me strongly. It was even worse since I still hadn't heard from Mac. I understood what Taz was telling me. They were doing something dangerous today and couldn't be distracted. But dammit, I needed him.

A sob caught in my throat and I squeezed my eyes closed as I covered my mouth with my hand to try to contain the sound.

"Knock, knock."

Donna's quiet voice had me dashing the tears away and taking a deep breath, desperately trying to get my shit together before I turned to look at where she stood by the curtain that separated us from the rest of the ER.

"Hey, Donna."

Her gaze ran over my face as she spoke. "Can I come in?"

With a wince, I gave her a nod as I wondered what the hell to say to her. Guilt ate at me that I'd been so harsh with her earlier that she was now questioning her welcome. Without another word, she came and sat in the chair next to mine. Her silence did my head in and I rushed to fill the void.

"Listen, Donna, I'm so sorry—"

"Don't be silly. You have nothing to apologize for, honey. I understand. I really do. You're a grown-ass woman and I got a little carried away being a mother hen on you. Should be me apologizing."

More tears sprung to my eyes and I sniffled as I tried to suck them back. She was being way too nice about this. She had every right to be angry. With me for lashing out, and with the club for making her stay with me in the first place.

"Not sure what the hell is wrong with me, but my emotions are all over the damn place. I've been flipping between hating the club and loving it lately. Today, I'm missing Mac like you read about, but I can't even call him."

She nodded. "And they forced me and Keys into your space without even asking you first, I'm guessing. These men of ours forget so easily that we women can actually take care of ourselves. I guess I'm so used to them now, I didn't stop to think you might not want or need our help." She paused on a sigh. "Club life isn't for the weak, that's for sure. But when the chips are down, I wouldn't want anyone else at my back than the club. When Emma did what she did, they could have kicked me and Keys to the curb over it. They certainly didn't have to step up like they did. You know the club covered all her funeral costs?"

I shook my head. Donna's daughter, Emma, had sold me out to the Iron Hammers MC, helping them kidnap me from the Charon MC clubhouse. Once they had me, they'd killed her and left her body for the club to find. It'd been a hell of a mess. Emma had gotten into drugs and her biological father, Sledge, who had been president of the Iron Hammers, had used his daughter without care to get what he wanted. Which had been me.

Emma had been a young, confused woman who'd sadly not gotten the chance to learn from her mistakes. No one, myself included, had ever laid any blame on Donna or Keys for what happened. The blame was firmly on Sledge's shoulders for the whole thing.

"Donna, there wasn't a damn thing about that situation that was your fault. You're not still feeling guilty over that, are you? Is that why you're always so fast to help me?"

My gut tightened that I'd been nothing but someone Donna had felt she had to help. I risked a glance in her direction and caught the sad smile that crossed her expression as she watched Cleo.

"Maybe to start with it was. Hell, maybe it still is part of it. But it's not the main reason. I like you, Zara. I'd like the think we're friends. And Cleo is such a little doll. I love spending time with you both. I hope I haven't ruined that with overstepping earlier today."

Grateful she wasn't only here out of guilt, I leaned over to bump my shoulder against hers. "We're good.

And thank you for all your help while Mac's been away. I really do appreciate it."

"Just an idea on why your emotions might be a little all over the place, but have you spoken to anyone about what happened at Marie's Cafe?"

I frowned and glanced at her again. "No. Why?"

"Honey, you were held at gunpoint. Shots were fired around you as you lay on the floor of the cafe. Just like what happened back in Galveston. That kind of thing is bound to hit some triggers for you, and then Mac getting dragged away to deal with club shit so soon after? You're allowed to need a minute to process it all."

"Huh. I hadn't really thought about that. But you're right. In a way, the shooting in Galveston was different. Thankfully I wasn't stuck under a dead man this time."

With a dash of humor in her voice, Donna spoke. "Bet you wish you had Cindy there that first time too, huh?"

That made me chuckle. "I'm so pissed off I missed seeing her come in all Harley Quinn like she did. The men were trying to be mad at her, but I could tell from their voices they were impressed as hell."

"She got the job done, that's for sure."

I let out a sigh. "When Mac gets back, I'll talk to him about it. Decompress. Hopefully that'll help me get level again. This emotional ping pong is wearing me the hell out."

"Good idea, and I bet it is. Has the Doc told you when they're releasing Cleo yet?"

I shook my head. "They were waiting to see if she needed another round of meds. She's looking so much better already, so I'm hoping she won't need any more and we can get home before too much longer."

"Hopefully. Let me go see what I can find out. If you want, I'll come home with ya'll?"

I smiled up at her as she stood. "That would be great. We'll order some pizzas and load up a movie or two."

I didn't want to sleep tonight, I wanted to watch Cleo to make sure she remained okay, but I didn't say that out loud because I knew as well as Donna did, that my narcolepsy wouldn't allow me to do it.

"Sounds like a plan. We'll take shifts watching your girl so we can both get some rest before morning."

Tears pricked my eyes again as she ducked out past the curtain. Yep, I might be pissed off that Mac was out of touch with me when I needed him so much, but I really couldn't stay mad with the club when they'd brought people like Donna into my life.

I suspected she was onto something with the shooting at the cafe. I hadn't really thought about it, hadn't really had time with how hectic everything had been since it had happened. Maybe I'd talk to her more about later tonight. See if that helped me feel better tomorrow.

Chapter 7

Mac

The half hour it took to break the fucker felt like hours. Jazz wrote down every detail that spilled from his lips once we did. By the time he started talking, he was so far gone he babbled every fucking thing in his head. We had pages of information we needed to go through. I doubted all of it was even true. He'd been a fucking mess by this point.

I was actually tempted to leave the fucker alive. He'd spend the rest of his days in an institution, a lifetime of suffering inside his own skin. But no, that would raise too many questions about how he got to be in the condition he was currently in.

"Blade, you end him."

I figured he'd earned the right to be able to put him down. When he put the tip of his blade to Sabella's chest I called out to him.

"No bone damage."

"I know. Got my name for a reason. I know exactly where to slice."

Sabella didn't react to the sight of the knife about to dig into his flesh at all. That's how far gone he was, too much electricity through his body and brain having done its job. Blade ran his fingers over Sabella's chest, locating ribs before he drove his blade in between two and straight into his heart. Seconds later, the bastard was dead.

"Let's do this. All the bodies need to be in their car. I'll grab the gas. Make it fast, men. We got people to save. Jazz, research those addresses for us. Give me a list of the most likely location he'd have held women."

I kept my eye on Blade as we got them moved. He was on edge and I wasn't sure how long I'd be able to hold him back. I understood where he was coming from. I remember how it had felt knowing that fucker, Sledge, had taken Zara and I hadn't known where they were. I also remember how I took off as soon as I did know. So far, Blade was sticking to the plan, but I knew that wouldn't hold. At some point, he'd go AWOL.

When we had the van loaded up and in the drive ready to head out, Eagle and I headed back to the cabin and car and lit up the fires that would cover our tracks. The flames shot up fast and hot due to all the accelerant we'd poured over everything. We sprinted for the van and Arrow hit the accelerator the moment we had the doors closed.

"The wind changed on us about ten minutes ago, the fire is heading this way now. Between what we just did and the wildfire, our tracks should be covered."

"It'll be interesting to see how the authorities play it once they figure out Sabella is one of the bodies in that car."

I agreed with Arrow. The next few days we'd be watching the news like hawks.

"What did you find out on those addresses, Jazz?"

He put in an address to the GPS for Arrow as he spoke. "I sent them through to Keys and he's sent back which one he thinks is the most likely to be what we're after."

Because by the time he gave us address, he was rambling and none of us were sure what addresses were what businesses. Jazz did the right thing pulling in Keys, our resident tech guy. He'd probably hacked into a satellite or some shit to go look at the addresses.

"Blade, what's the deal with this cop you got to take the victims?"

"We go in first and clear it out, then I'll call her. I've got some payback to do before we have the boys in blue there to curb our fun."

I scrubbed a palm over my face. This was going to be a long day and I had no clue who was going to be left standing at the end of it. Blade was now a wild card who could change the game at any moment. But I couldn't knock him out and go in without him. I knew what he was feeling right now, and I knew he'd never forgive me if I didn't allow him to do this.

By the time we parked down the street from the warehouse Keys was certain was our target, we were all back in the zone. Armed up and ready to fight. No tranqs this time, only live ammo all around.

"Arrow and Eagle, you go ahead and take out any guards. When you send me the all clear, we'll come in."

With nods, they slipped free from the van and jogged down the street. It was late afternoon but I wished it were night. With the cover of darkness, their jobs would be a lot easier. Although the smoke did give us some cover. It wasn't as thick here as it had been at the cabin, but it was still heavy in the air. Blade shifted in his seat.

"Soon, Blade. We need to do this right so we don't end up with more causalities than necessary."

I wasn't sure if I wanted to find his girl alive or not. If what Sabella had told us was the truth, she'd been put through hours of the worst abuse a woman could be put through. At a guess, if she was alive, she'd be wishing she wasn't by now. More images flickered across my mind, not just of my sister's dead body but also of Zara's as we'd found her. Hanging from a hook, naked and whipped raw from her shoulders down over her ass. She still bore the physical scars from that day, and we both bore the mental ones. The possibility that there were women and fucking children being put through that same thing just up the road from us was doing my head in. But like I'd told Blade, we couldn't simply storm the place. We were no doubt outnumbered in this situation, and those men didn't care about the women and kids they had under their control. They'd use them as shields in a heartbeat.

My phone beeped with the all clear message from Arrow.

"We're good to go in."

Jazz had moved to the driver's seat when Arrow had left earlier and now he started the van up and drove us toward the warehouse. We parked away from the entrance, to lessen the chances of anyone inside hearing the engine. Then we were jogging over to where Eagle and Arrow had their weapons trained on the side door.

"Took out four men guarding the exterior. They weren't on high alert."

"They were too easy to take out. Bastards weren't paying any attention to their surroundings."

"That works in our favor. If they're not expecting trouble, we should be able to slip in and get this done quickly." I paused to take a deep breath. "You all know the plan. Watch your backs, stay safe and let's get this done."

Blade went up to the door and swung it open to reveal an empty hallway. We all fell in behind him, except for Jazz, who stayed outside to cover the exit for us. My heart was pounding in my chest like it used to do when we were on a mission over in the Middle East. I thought my days of doing this shit were over when I retired from the USMC, had been happy to put it behind me. But to keep innocents safe, I'd do it time and again without hesitation. If I could spare even one woman from the hell my sister was put through leading up to her death, I'm there to help.

The first door we came across was locked with a heavy slide bolt lock, Blade slid it across and after checking we had him covered, swung the door open. We'd put Blade out front in the hopes that when we found Sabella's men, they'd recognize him and not shoot straight away, thus giving us time to put them down without getting injured ourselves.

The smell that rushed out over us was horrific and left me struggling to not gag as Blade cursed. The small room had maybe a dozen kids and teens all jammed in there. They were all naked and dirty. I tried not to focus on the dried blood that was mixed in with the filth on them. In the seconds it took the rest of us to shake free from our shock, Bank took control and moved past Blade into the room.

"Don't be scared. We're here to help you. But before we can take you out of here, we need to lock you back in for just a little bit longer, okay? We need to take out the men who put you in here, then we'll be back to get you out of here."

One of the older teens detangled herself from the younger children she was holding to her.

"If you're really here to help us, give me a weapon. They could come back while you're gone."

Bank looked to me with an eyebrow raised. Fuck, I didn't want to arm the kid but I couldn't deny the point she made. I unstrapped one of my knives and step forward past Bank to hand it to her, handle first.

"I really don't want to have to hurt you, so please don't turn that on any of us. We truly are here to rescue you."

This kid had steel in her that was for sure. She nodded as she took the weapon. We left the room and when I glanced back to her before Blade re-shut the door, I saw her standing strong with a death grip on that knife of mine as she stared back at me.

Without another word, we kept moving down the hallway. The sounds of men enjoying sex filled the air. Fuckers were cheering and having a grand time by the sounds of it, and Blade was about to levitate with all the rage pouring off him. We reached the door that, from the noise level, had to be where the men were.

"Everyone loaded and ready?"

I glanced at all the men to see everyone was locked and loaded, weapons on the door.

"Do it, Blade."

He shoved the door open hard and fast and the thunder of gunshots filled the air as we all took our shots. None of us fired aimlessly, we carefully chose our targets before we squeezed off rounds, dropping the men who surrounded a woman on a table. The last man standing pulled the woman up against his front, a knife to her throat as he shielded himself behind the woman he'd just been violating. Blade's agonized scream tore through me as he raced forward, completely disregarding his personal safety. I was on him in seconds, holding him back as I spoke into his ear.

"Stop and think. He'll kill her."

The noise that came from his throat reminded me of a wounded, dying animal, but I didn't release him. Blade obviously hadn't noticed what Eagle was doing, and neither had the fucker holding his girl hostage. Eagle used the commotion that Blade caused to slip around the perimeter of the room and get behind Sabella's man. Before the fucker knew what hit him, Eagle slammed a knife into the back of his neck. He dropped, dead, and Eagle caught the barely-conscious woman in his arms before she could fall with him. I released Blade the moment I saw the life leave Sabella's man's eyes and he was across the room and taking the woman from Eagle in moments. With her cradled against him, he sank to the floor, stroking her face as he rested his forehead against hers. He was whispering to her but I couldn't hear what he was saying.

Arrow came up next to me. "We need to clear the rest of the building. There's gotta be more women somewhere, and I've got no idea if there's more men in with them."

"I know, brother. Give me a minute."

I moved over to Blade and crouched beside where he sat on the floor with his girl now unconscious in his arms. She was in a bad way, her body battered more than my sister's had been when she'd been murdered. I had no clue if she was still alive. Slowly, I leaned over and pressed two fingers to her throat, moving around, looking for a pulse.

"Don't say it."

She'd just died in his arms. And he knew it.

"I'm sorry, brother. But we gotta keep moving. We need to find the other women and any other men who are here. We can lock you in here and come back for you—"

He cut me off with a shake of his head. "I want blood for this. No way am I fucking going to sit this one out."

On shaky legs, he stood and rested his girl gently on the table before pressing a kiss to her temple and whispering something too quiet for us to hear. My eyes stung at the agony he was feeling. It was too close to the pain I felt after my sister's murder and both times Zara was taken from me. I briefly squeezed his shoulder before I turned and left the room.

Taking point, I led my team the rest of the way down to the end of the hallway. Reaching for the door, I held my breath, unsure if I was ready for what was waiting us. With my gun up, ready to fire, I shoved the door open and took in what I found. Thin walls had the space within this main area of the warehouse broken up into small cubicles. There were curtains on each one, but only a couple of them were closed. The open ones revealed naked women cuffed to beds.

Using hand gestures, I indicated the need to clear out the closed off spaces. Since there were no men on guard, I guessed those who should have been guarding had all left their posts to go get busy with Blade's girl. We each lined up with a closed curtain and I counted down with a hand in the air from three to one. At once, we all tore back the curtains at the same time, shooting the fuckers we found with one shot to the head.

A couple of the women shrieked at the sounds of the gunshots but most of them were too far gone on drugs to react. Or too beaten down to care. Leaving the women for now, we continued to sweep the entire space, looking for more of Sabella's men. All we found was an office with way too much paperwork for my liking. We also found a handful of handcuff keys in there. Once we established that there were no more active threats we went back to the women and after I passed around the keys, we started unlocking their cuffs.

"Blade, call in your contacts. Bank, go get Jazz and get those kids and bring them here."

Blade walked away with his phone out as Arrow came over to me. "What do you want to do with this place?"

"I was thinking if we can get all the women and kids out in the parking lot, we can light this shit in the office up, burn it all so whoever is left of Sabella's crew can't restart this operation back up. I'd love to burn the whole fucking place to the ground, but that's not feasible, or safe."

Blade strode back into the room. "She's given us twenty minutes to get outta here. She's going to call in for a bus and ambulances for the women and kids. We need to be gone before then."

The kids came in behind Blade, with Jazz bringing up the rear. Three of the kids ran for separate women that we'd just freed. My heart hurt for every one of these kids and women. Fuck. The more women we freed, the more kids went running. When I noticed the eldest teen didn't even go looking, I went over to her and the closer I got, the tighter her grip got on the knife, to the point her knuckles were white. Reaching over my head, I pulled my t-shirt off and held it out to her. Her eyes went wide before narrowing on me.

"Take it. I mean you no harm. We're here to rescue you all, not hurt you."

She snatched it from me and without taking her gaze off me, slipped it over her head, keeping my knife firmly in her grip as she threaded her arms through the armholes.

"Is one of these women your mom?"

The glint of rage in her eyes had me holding my hands up. "I was only asking so I could help you find her if she was."

The kid was killing me. She was clearly strong and she hadn't let these bastards break her. She reminded me so much of Zara. Even naked and beaten, she stood tall, ready to go into battle.

"My mom was the one who sold me to these assholes. If she's here, I don't give a fuck."

Son of a bitch. This poor girl. "Fair enough. Think you can help us get everyone outside? We need to torch that room at the back so no one can come in and find the information that would allow them to start this shit back up."

Fury flashed across her dark eyes before she lifted her chin and gave me a solid nod. Then she marched forward toward the kids and women. The kids all listened to her as she spoke. They obviously trusted her. With how she was acting now, I'd guess she took more than a few beatings trying to protect the younger ones. With a few words from her, the kids began to tug at their moms, trying to get them to move. The women who were able, started moving toward the door, the ones too far gone we set about carrying out. Joining the other men, I wrapped a woman in a sheet, before I lifted her up and headed toward the large garage door that had now been opened to the outside. The sun was heading toward the horizon, and the smoke in the air made everything a strange, orange color as the sun began to set. It was eerie as fuck.

Between the five of us, we got everyone out into the parking lot in about fifteen minutes. When we were nearly done, I sent Blade to go to the van to get what he needed to light up the office. If the whole building burned, it was no loss. All we cared about was making sure that everything inside that fucking office burned to ash. Once I was done moving the last woman, I headed back to toward the office. Understandably, Blade wasn't right after what happened to his girl and I wanted to make sure he didn't do anything stupidly reckless.

I was about three quarters of the way to the rear of the main warehouse space when I heard the whoosh of flames followed by Blade's curses.

Unsure what was going on, I snatched a blanket off one of the beds and sprinted for the office. Blade stumbled backwards out of the room, flames licking up his side.

"Fuck."

Throwing the blanket over the flames, I shoved him down onto the ground and rolled him until the flames were out. The moment they were, I had him over my shoulder and was gunning for the exit. When I hit the parking lot, I saw that the van had been backed up to the entrance and the engine was running. Arrow stepped up to open the side door.

"Get him to a hospital. Jazz and Bank will come back for Eagle and me. We'll make sure it's the police who pick these ladies and kids up, not more of Sabella's men, then we'll meet up back at the trailer."

"You sure?"

I didn't want to risk anyone's safety but Blade needed medical attention ASAP. And Arrow was right, we couldn't risk the wrong people finding these women and kids.

"Yeah, we'll make sure we're well hidden with the authorities arrive. Jazz knows where to pick us up. Go get your boy taken care of. At least with all these wildfires, they won't ask too many questions about the how of his burns."

I nodded and after setting Blade down across the rear seats, I made myself comfortable on the floor near him. Arrow closed the door, then we were off. As we raced down the road, I placed my hands on his uninjured side to keep him still as Jazz raced around corners to get us where we needed to be. Blade was keeping stoically silent, but the set of his jaw and his eyes gave away the amount of pain he was suffering.

"We'll get you taken care of, brother."

He gave me a small nod but stayed silent.

I wanted to say so much, but had no fucking clue where to start. My main concern was that this hadn't been an accident and he'd tried to take himself out but the pain had been more than he'd anticipated and had sent him retreating from that office before the job was done. Ultimately, I guess it didn't matter, right now. I'd make sure he got the medical help he needed, then I'd make sure he got better, even if I had to drag his ass back to Texas with me.

Sparrow

My whole life, I've never known what to expect to come at me from one day to the next. The only thing I could be certain of was that it was likely to be bad. Nothing had been as bad as the past however long it had been since my mom sold me to her dealer to clear her debt, though. I'd never bothered to keep track of the days passing. Hadn't seen the point in it. So I had no clue how long I'd been stuck in that horrible warehouse.

One thing I did do, and never stopped doing, was fighting those bastards. They never *ever* got anything from me without paying for it with their flesh. I'd scratch, bite, kick, punch. Whatever I could do, I did. No matter the consequences, I never stopped fighting. For me, or the other kids. At fifteen, I was the oldest they had in the "pedo room." Most of the sick perverts who paid for the right to abuse a child wanted someone younger, someone less likely to fight back. Sucked to be them, because I didn't care who they'd set their sights on, I fought them all. There wasn't one child in that room who I hadn't fought for.

A tremor ran through my body as memories of all the times my fighting did nothing but delay the inevitable. I'd no doubt had more concussions than was healthy from all the blows to the head I'd taken, not to mention my arm that hadn't healed right and still ached. And those poor kids, some just toddlers, still got taken and abused before being tossed back to me to try to put back together again. The assholes that ran the place laughed every time I fought. Told me they only kept me around because they didn't want to deal with the kids after they got used. And the fact some of the men they brought in wanted someone older.

I shuddered again.

My life had been hell.

When that man had barged into the room earlier, I'd been ready to fight again. Always hopeful that maybe this time I could make them go away without taking anyone.

Then I'd seen the other men and my heart had dropped. No way could I take that many on, but they'd stopped short. They hadn't looked at any of us with lust in their eyes. Instead, they'd looked mortified. Then the big, bald man had given me a weapon and they'd told us they'd be back to free us. Unfortunately they'd also locked us back up, so I hadn't been able to escape either on my own or with the others. That had driven me nuts. I'd wanted out so bad.

But they'd kept their word and had come back for us. I still wasn't sure what to make of them as they led us to the main room of the warehouse. Some of the younger kids had run screaming to their moms, and as the men released more of the women from the beds they'd been locked to, more kids found their moms. I couldn't help my reaction to seeing those beds. I'd been told that's where I'd go once I aged out of the pedo room. They'd even brought me in here a few times to watch what happened. Telling me if I didn't quit fighting every man that came for me, I'd end up here sooner rather than later. But even with that threat over me, I just couldn't not fight. It wasn't in my nature to lie down and let life fuck me over.

The big, bald guy who seemed to be in charge came at me, stripping off his shirt. I'd held my breath and tightened my grip on the knife still in my hand, but the strike I'd been expecting never came. Instead, he'd been nice. Giving me the shirt to cover up my nudity that I'd forgotten about. None of us ever had clothes here. He was so tall that his shirt covered me nearly to my knees. I rolled my shoulders and shuddered at the strange sensation of having material against my skin for the first time in so long.

After I helped get the remaining kids and the women who could walk outside, I looked around, assessing the situation. I'd heard them talking and knew authorities were coming to collect everyone. I also knew I couldn't be here when they arrived. They'd give me back to my mom, or worse, find my dad and give me to him. Neither of those options were ones I could live with. So I'd stood there, off to the side from everyone else and watched our rescuers in action. Each man was gentle with the women they carried out from the warehouse, settling each one carefully before returning for another.

When I'd scanned the parking lot earlier, I'd noticed what must be their van parked off to the rear. Checking everyone was still busy and focused elsewhere, I'd slipped into the evening shadows and made my way over toward it. Of all my options, those men seemed like the safest bet to get me away from here. Testing the rear door, I'd found it thankfully unlocked, so with my breath held, I'd slipped inside. Making sure the door was shut tight once more, I took in the back of the vehicle in the fading sunlight. There were three rows of seats, including the driver and front passenger seat, then the back of the van was mostly empty storage space. A smile tugged at my lips when I'd seen a few blankets shoved to the side near where I was. I'd crawled over and covered myself with them, making sure nothing of me showed but I'd still had an opening near my face so I could breathe.

I hadn't been there long when I'd heard the doors open and close and the engine start up. I had no idea what had happened, but after the vehicle drove a short way, it stopped again and the side door opened. All the men seemed panicked as one told the others to get a man to the hospital, I couldn't hear all the words spoken through the blankets but I had started to wonder how good my plan really was when the van took off in a rush. I struggled to hold my place under the blankets as the van raced around corners faster than I thought it was supposed to.

When it screeched to a stop, I nearly cried out as I slid forward, only just catching myself with my hand before my head slammed into the back of the rear seats. Sirens and bright lights filled the van and I made fast work of re-hiding myself, hoping and praying that no one had seen me.

"No way to do this without it hurting, Blade."

"Just do it already."

Oh no, one of the rescuers had gotten hurt. I had no idea which man was Blade, but the other man who'd spoken was the one who'd given me his shirt. That made me feel safer. He'd been nice to me. Even if they did discover me now, I was hopeful he wouldn't take me back to that warehouse for the cops to deal with. I'd hoped that I could stay hidden until they drove far away from that place. Until it was too late to turn back around.

Although I had realized I'd had no clue where they were going. For all I knew they could live just down the road from where I'd been held.

I hoped not.

I hoped that they lived far, far away and they didn't notice me back here until they got there.

Squeezing my eyes tightly closed, I'd blocked out all the noises around me and prayed they didn't find me yet. That this crazy plan would work out and I'd be able to start over somewhere everyone didn't want to hurt me or watch me be hurt.

Chapter 8

Mac

Even when we'd all made it safely back to Blade's trailer, I'd still hadn't been able to relax. Something was wrong but I'd been unable to put my finger on it. Blade was out cold thanks to the pain meds the hospital had pumped into him. His jeans had taken the brunt of the heat on his lower half but his arm had been a real mess. His face had caught a little heat but thankfully not seriously burned. The doc had told us that my quick thinking with the blanket had most likely saved at the least his arm, if not his life. That got me thinking again about whether Blade's accident with spilling gas on himself had truly been an accident. But my gut told me this nagging feeling I had wasn't about Blade. Something else was going on.

"You checked in with Scout yet?"

I shook my head then looked to Arrow. "Not yet. My instincts are screaming at me. But I'm not sure why yet."

"Give him a call."

I frowned at him. "What do you know that I don't, brother?"

He just nodded at my pocket where my phone was. "Just make the call, Mac."

I hated this vague bullshit, and it was fucking strange, coming from Arrow. Normally the man shot straight from the hip and didn't waste time with games.

With a growl, I ripped my phone from my pocket and pulled up the secure app, and pressed Scout's number.

"Hit me."

Scout sounded more tired than usual, another sign something more was going on.

"It's done. Sabella is dead, his stable is cleaned out and the victims are all in the hands of the authorities."

"Injuries?"

"Blade got burned up his right side. Dropped some gas down himself and a spark caught him. He's gotten medical attention but I want to bring him back with us. Sabella had his woman. Blade thought she'd been killed years ago, but Sabella had her the whole time. We found her in the warehouse. They'd been using her hard and she died in his arms after we killed the fuckers. I'm worried about him."

"You don't think he accidentally spilled the gas, do you?"

I scrubbed a hand over my face. "I'm not sure. But that's my suspicion."

Scout was quiet for a minute.

"Make sure he's on board with coming with you. If he's good with relocating, he's welcome here. Up to him if he wants to try his hand at club life. We'll discuss it further if he decides to come home with you. Speaking of which, when you planning on heading back?"

My senses kicked up again. There was something about his voice that had me standing straighter.

"As soon as Blade's ready to travel. Why? What's happening?"

He sighed heavily enough I heard it over the line. "Guessing you haven't called your woman yet?"

"No, I was checking in with you first. She's my next call. Why?"

"Good. You need to call her."

Ignoring the fact he was my president, I growled at him while glaring at Arrow. "Fucking tell me what's going on. You and Arrow clearly know something I don't, and it's screwing with my head."

Scout's voice dropped to a growl. "Remember who you're talking to, brother."

"I will as soon as ya'll stop fucking with me and tell me straight what the fuck is going on."

"Fine! Cleo wasn't teething. It was an ear infection. The doc gave her amoxicillin and it turns out she's allergic—"

Panic had my heart rate racing. "Is Cleo all right? Is Zara? And why the fuck am I just hearing about this now?"

"Calm the fuck down. They're both fine. Well, Zara's mad as hell at the club because we sent you away then told her not to call you when it all went down earlier. But health-wise, they're both fine. Donna and Keys are with them at your place."

"I'm not exactly happy she wasn't allowed to call either."

"Seriously? Think that through, brother. You were raiding that fucking warehouse. You really think hearing that your daughter was in the hospital would have helped you stay focused? There wasn't shit you could do about it, so we decided it was safer to wait. Now quit chewing my ass about this and go call your woman. Let me know when you're leaving."

He hung up before I could say another word. As I pulled up Zara's number, I glared at Arrow. "You could have told me."

"I didn't know enough details to tell you. All I knew was that something was up with Cleo and you needed to call home once we were done here. Telling you that would have just stressed you out more. Head out the back and give her a call, brother. No point in wasting your time or energy on being mad at something none of us can go back and change."

I didn't bother trying to say anything else to him before I spun on my heel and stormed out of the rear of the trailer. I got why the club had prevented Zara from calling me earlier, but that didn't change the fact I was fucking furious that I was so far away from my family when they'd needed me. Zara's narcolepsy and cataplexy had improved since she'd given birth. She figured it was because her maternal instinct trumped her illnesses but I'd bet she was still struggling.

A quick glance at the time had me wincing. It was past ten pm back home but I couldn't wait till morning to speak to her. Hitting dial, I held my phone to my ear and prayed she was still awake and wasn't so mad she wouldn't answer my call.

Zara

With Cleo sleeping in my arms, I watched a movie with Donna and Keys, and had a big talk about that day at Marie's Cafe with them. Feeling drained but with a clearer head, I'd headed upstairs to put Cleo down while Donna and Keys had gone to bed. I'd assured them I was heading to bed too but I couldn't sleep so I was sitting here in Cleo's room, watching her little body rise and fall with each breath when my phone buzzed in my pocket. Without taking my gaze from Cleo, I pulled it out, then after a quick glance showed me it was Mac, I'd answered it as fast as I could. Thankfully, Cleo slept like the dead once she was out so I didn't bother leaving her room before I spoke.

"Hey."

"Hey, bunny. I hear you've had a busy day. Wanna fill me in?"

A flash of anger heated my face. "So you've already called Scout, then?"

"Sweetheart, don't get mad. I rang him first so I could talk with you for longer. If I'd called you first, I would have had to make it quick so I could go ring him. Now, we have all night to talk. If you want."

I huffed out a breath and forced myself to calm down.

"I hate that you're not here. I needed you."

"I hate I wasn't there when you needed me, too. Tell me what happened, bunny."

"Cleo got worse after you left. By this morning I knew it wasn't her teeth, so I took her to the doctor. She's got an ear infection. Dr. Stevenson wasn't worried, neither was Donna. They both said kids get them all the time and she'd be fine with some medicine. But she was allergic to the amoxicillin they had me give her. I was watching her pretty closely and when I noticed she had a rash, I ran over to Taz and Flick's place and he drove me to the hospital, where they treated her."

Tears pricked my eyes thinking about it all.

"Oh, sweetheart, I'm so sorry I wasn't there for you both. So, baby girl's allergic to penicillin, yeah? Anything we need to do in the future for that?"

I shrugged, even though he couldn't see me. "I'll go in with her for a check-up in a couple days and ask, but I don't think so. Maybe get her one of those medic alert bracelet things when she's a bit older? Not sure. For now, the whole club knows about her allergy and it's listed on her records at the hospital."

"Fuck. I wish I was home and could wrap you both up in my arms."

I swiped at my tears. I wanted that too. So badly.

"Do you know when you're coming home yet?"

"Hopefully we can head back first thing in the morning. I'll try to convince the boys to ride through the night so we can get home faster."

My heart melted a little that he was so desperate to get back to us. "Staying safe and making it home in one piece is more important than getting home faster, babe."

"Yeah, I know. I won't be stupid about it. I'm hoping I can get Blade to come with us. He's gonna need someone watching his back and I'm not comfortable leaving him here."

There was a strain to his voice that had me worried. I knew he wouldn't discuss what they'd been doing, which was perfectly fine with me. I was fairly certain I didn't want to know. But I did want to know what was going on with Blade. Mac didn't speak of him often, but I knew they'd been close back when Mac had been caught up in the mob.

"What's wrong with Blade?"

A heavy sigh came over the line. "I'll explain it more when I get home, but he lost someone he cared for and in the process ended up with some nasty burns."

"Bring him home. We'll take care of him."

He was silent for a moment before he cleared his throat. "Love you so much, Zara. Best old lady ever."

Heat raced over my cheeks. "Love you too, babe. But I'm not so sure about being the best old lady. I've been cursing the club a lot this past week."

He chuckled. "I bet you have. But I bet you were grateful for them just as much. I mean, Taz dropped everything to get you and Cleo to the hospital, right?"

"Yeah, and Donna went with me to see Dr. Stevenson. It's been an emotional roller coaster of a week. I'm not sure how I feel about anything, at this point. Well, except for you and Cleo. I love you both to the moon and back."

I didn't mention about how the cafe shooting was affecting me. He didn't need that added stress right now and I wanted to talk to him about that in person, not over the phone.

"Ditto, bunny. Hate being so far from you. Listen, I gotta go. Need to get some sleep before the long ride home tomorrow. You make sure you get some sleep too. No spending the night in the chair in Cleo's room. You'll be wrecked tomorrow if you do."

My face heated with embarrassment that he knew what I'd intended to do. "But I need to keep an eye on her."

"Zara, baby, if she needed to be watched that closely, they would have kept her in the hospital. Turn the baby monitor on and take that into our room with you. Go get some real sleep, not the shit sleep you'll get sitting in that chair. We both know your narcolepsy won't let you stay awake all night, so go get comfortable in our bed and try to relax. I'll be home as soon as I can."

Gah, I hated it when he made so much sense. I couldn't argue with any of his points. He was right. Not that I'd admit it to him.

"Fine. You go get some sleep too, and let me know when you're heading out. I can't wait to see you."

We said our goodbyes and love yous before ending the call. Then I went and grabbed the baby monitor we hadn't used in months and set it back up before heading for our bedroom to try to sleep.

By the time Cleo was about three months old, she'd holler loud enough for the whole damn street to hear when she wanted something during the night, so we hadn't bothered with the monitor. But tonight, I was grateful we'd kept it. I actually felt silly for not thinking of it before Mac mentioned it. I hadn't been looking forward to how I'd feel tomorrow after sleeping in that chair in her room.

Chapter 9

Mac

After a restless night of not getting much sleep, I was up at dawn to try to get everyone sorted so we could leave. I'd told everyone except for Blade about Cleo after my phone call, so they all knew why I was so damn anxious to get on the road.

I went into the room we'd put Blade in last night to see him thrashing in his sleep.

"Blade! Wake up, man."

I didn't touch him, as I had no clue how that would go over. I knew men who'd kill someone who touched them while they slept, purely out of reflex.

With a groan, he reached his left hand up and rubbed his face, wincing when his fingers caught the edge of a burn. The side of his neck, ear and a small part of his cheek were red from the fire. It wasn't a serious burn like up his arm thankfully, but it was gonna sting when he touched it for a while.

He blinked up at me.

"What's going on?"

"We got a lot to discuss, and not a whole lot of time at the moment to do it, so I'm gonna keep it brief. I'm not comfortable leaving you alone right now. I don't like where your head's at after yesterday. I wish I could offer to stay here with you, but that's a no go. Got word from home last night that my baby girl's been in the hospital. I need to get home to my family and I want you to come with us."

He winced and moved his gaze to the ceiling.

"I ain't one of you, Mac. I don't belong—"

"Bull fucking shit, Blade! You belong. You've helped out the Charons more than once. I have Scout's blessing to bring you back to Bridgewater. He told me it was up to you if you wanted to join the club, but even if you don't, you're welcome in our town. My old lady told me last night to bring you home so we could look after you." I paused until he turned his gaze back to me. "You're not alone, brother. Let us help you. Once your burns heal up, we'll revisit where you want to live going forward. If you want to come back here, you can. If you don't, we'll help you move all your shit to Bridgewater."

He stayed quiet for a minute.

"What's up with your kid?"

"Allergic reaction to amoxicillin. Zara got her to hospital in time so she'll be fine, but I wanna get back home to them to see for myself."

Before I could get an answer out of Blade, Jazz came tearing through the trailer and skidding through the bedroom door as though the hounds of hell were on his heels.

"We got a problem, Mac. A big, fucking problem."

I frowned his way as several options on what might have him riled up passed through my mind. Reaching for my gun, I headed out of Blade's room.

"Spill it, Jazz. What the fuck's going on?"

"Nothing that needs a gun. At least I hope that's not the route we're taking...."

"Jazz. Cut the shit. What is the problem?"

"We got a stowaway. That teenager from the warehouse—the one you gave your shirt to—well, she's asleep in the back of the van."

Putting my gun back in its holster, I headed for the front door, cursing. This was the last thing we needed.

"She still sleeping?"

"Yeah, I saw her through the window as I was about to open things up. Figured I'd get you before I risked waking her."

Once at the van, I peeked through the window and sure enough, the little spitfire teen from yesterday was curled up asleep in the rear of the van. The pile of blankets half covered her. She must have hidden herself beneath them yesterday but had moved out from under them as she'd slept.

"Open it up, Jazz. Let's get this dealt with."

Everyone was out at the van now. Even Blade had managed to drag his sorry looking self outside. I looked to Arrow and he nodded to the van, letting me this was all mine. Great fucking time for Scout to put me in charge of a run.

When the door opened the kid jerked awake, and after a moment grabbed the blankets.

"We know you're there, darlin'."

She turned wide eyes toward us, running her gaze over each of us before settling on me.

"Please. Don't send me back."

Fury laced through my system. "I'd never send anyone back to a place like that. We busted that shit wide open and burned it to the ground so no one could ever be sent back there."

She shook her head. "Not the warehouse, to the cops."

I could see the fear in her eyes and knew this was going to take more than a minute to sort out.

"How about you come on inside? Get cleaned up and get something to eat, then we'll discuss what the next step here is gonna be."

Bank cleared his throat and I turned to face him.

"I'll head down to Walmart and grab her something to change into and some other stuff she'll need."

I gave him a nod. "Good idea. Thanks, brother." I turned back to the girl. "What size are you, darlin'?"

She rattled off her digits and Bank gave her a nod. "I've got you covered, honey. Got a baby sister who's probably about your age."

With that, Bank headed to his bike and took off. I held my hand out to her.

"C'mon, kid. Let's get you inside and more comfortable."

She hesitated for a moment before putting her dirty, bruised hand into mine. There was no way I could miss the scabs on her knuckles. Clearly, she'd fought hard against those fuckers who'd held her. And as much as it pained me that she'd been in that fucking warehouse to begin with, I was also rather proud that she'd kept up fighting them and hadn't just given up.

Sparrow

Nerves had me trembling as I took the hand he offered and left the back of the van. I hadn't meant to fall so deeply asleep. I couldn't remember the last time I'd slept so soundly that I hadn't been aware of what was around me, but I guess everything finally caught up with me and I passed the fuck out last night. The sun was only just peeking over the horizon and thanks to all the smoke in the air, everything was hazy and tainted dark red.

When my bare feet hit the ground I landed on a rock and pain flashed up my leg, sending my knee out as I gasped.

"I got you."

He swung me up into his arms and carried me inside, not setting me back down until he entered a small bathroom.

"Here you go. Take all the time you need, there's soap…" He paused as he opened the cupboard over the sink, then looked through the drawers beneath it. "New toothbrush. Let me go ask the others if they have any shampoo for you."

Before I could say a word he left me standing there. Alone, but safe. I knew I was being naive to think that, but these men had come storming into the warehouse and saved us all. They wouldn't do that just to turn on me now.

Hopefully.

Before I could get myself worked up, he returned holding a couple of bottles.

"Okay, I don't want to think about why Jazz had conditioner, but that works out well for you." He set the bottles down next to the sink. "Here's a towel. Take your time getting clean. Looks like it's been a while since you've had the chance. No one here is a threat to you in any way, okay? Once you're done, come on out and we'll get some food into you and discuss what we're gonna do."

The thought of a hot shower and food nearly made me dizzy with glee, but I was still scared of what would happen afterward. I reached out and gripped his arm.

"Please, don't send me back."

He tilted his head as he ran his gaze over my face. "What has you so scared of the cops?"

"It's not the cops so much as where they'll send me. I'll end up either back with my mother, who'll just sell me again, or with my father." A shudder ran through me. "Who, I'm told, would rather see me dead than in his home."

He let out a sigh.

"Take your shower, ah. What's your name?"

"Sparrow." I smiled as he frowned. "Yeah, as in the bird. Another little present from my mom. What's your name?"

"Ah, shit, we didn't introduce ourselves did we? I'm Mac, darlin'. I'll introduce the others when you get out. I'll have Bank leave your clothes just outside the door for you."

He nodded, then without another word, turned and left the room, closing the door behind him. I followed him and flipped the lock before returning to the shower. I pulled the curtain back and leaned in to flip on the tap. Fresh, clean water flowed instantly and I smiled while I set the bottles of shampoo and conditioner on the edge of the tub. Peeling off his shirt, I placed it over the edge of the sink before I put my hand under the water and adjusted the temperature. Once it was perfect, I stepped into the tub and groaned as the fresh water ran down over me. I couldn't remember the last time I'd been free to enjoy a hot shower.

Emotion clogged my throat and a sob broke free as I turned my face up and let the warm water wash my tears away. Mac had told me to take my time, and I fully intended to. Being able to safely release my tears and getting clean was simply too good to rush through.

When my skin was wrinkly and the water was starting to cool, I turned the taps off and stepped out onto the mat. Picking up the towel, I dried off and gave my hair a squeeze to get as much water as I could out of it. The curls had matted together and even after putting a heap of conditioner through it, I knew it was going to be a job to get it all brushed out. It would no doubt be easier to cut it all off, but I'd always loved my thick hair and really didn't want to lose it now.

Wrapping the towel around my torso, I crept over to the door and flicking the lock, carefully opened it. There were two bags sitting by the wall and I quickly snatched them before reclosing and locking the door. The trailer was small and I knew they would have seen me just now. Well, they would have seen my arm as I reached out. Taking the towel from my body, I wrapped it around my hair turban-style before kneeling on the mat to look in the bags.

I spent a while just touching it all. I was so overwhelmed I didn't even know what to think. It had been rare that I'd gotten anything new growing up. Standing up, I started getting dressed with the plain white, cotton panties. Then the sports bra. The stretchy material clung to me and instantly made me feel warmer and more secure. Diving back into the bag, I dragged out a pair of dark blue jeans and slipped them on, stretching my legs out some at how strange they felt. Had it really been that long since I'd worn clothes?

I shook my head, refusing to let my thoughts go there. Digging back into the bag, I found a tank. It was plain black with a big white skull on the front. It was smiling and had pretty hearts and swirls on it. I'd never seen anything like it but it made me smile, so I put it on before looking up into the mirror. More tears ran down my cheeks. I looked normal. Like the kids I'd seen on the street back before I was taken to the warehouse.

Back in the bags I found socks and really sturdy looking boots. After tugging the tag off, I looked at it. They were work boots, like with a steel-capped toe. If I kicked someone with these, it would really do them some damage. Was that why they bought them for me? To help me feel safe?

I didn't understand these men at all, but I was so grateful for them. There was more stuff in the bags. A few extra pieces of clothing, a small backpack, deodorant, brush, comb, some hair ties. Even some spray leave-in conditioner.

A knock on the door startled me.

"Sparrow? You okay in there, darlin'?"

That was when I realized I was crying again. I dashed the tears away and cleared my throat.

"I'm good, Mac. Just be another few minutes."

"Okay."

Quickly shoving everything except the brush, comb and conditioner into the backpack, I took the towel off my hair then headed for the door. Taking a deep breath, I flipped the lock once more before I opened the door. A quick glance showed me all the men were sitting around a table and they were all looking at me. Mac stood and came toward me.

"Come on out, Sparrow. Let me introduce everyone."

It was getting easier to put my faith in Mac. He looked like a hard-ass, but his eyes were gentle when he looked at me. And he'd yet to do a single thing to hurt me.

"Is it okay if I do my hair out here?"

He smiled. "Sure, darlin'. You make yourself right at home."

Gripping my new possessions tightly, I followed him over to the others.

Chapter 10

Mac

With my hands on my hips, I stared at the door to the bathroom. I'd heard her flip the lock a few minutes ago and now I could hear her crying over the sound of the shower. This kid was gutting me with her pain, and her strength.

Arrow came and stood beside me.

"She all right?"

"No fucking clue, brother."

"She tell you anything else?"

I nodded before turning to head over to the table where I sat. Within minutes the rest of the guys were all there sitting around me.

"Yesterday I asked her if her mom was in the warehouse. She told me straight out she didn't give a fuck if she was because the bitch had sold her daughter to pay off a drug debt. Just now she told me her dad would kill her before he'd take her into his home. I saw the shudder run through her at the thought of her old man. What the fuck, brothers? I don't understand how parents can do that."

The others were silent, because really, what could you say? The rumble of a bike preceded Bank's return with a couple bags of stuff.

"I told her you'd put her stuff by the door. She's locked it."

With a nod, he headed toward the bathroom before he returned and joined us.

Blade rapped the knuckles of his good hand on the table and I looked over to him.

"You want me to come back to Texas with you? Well, I'll do it, but only if we take her with us as well."

"What the fuck, man. That's not up to us! She's a fucking minor."

The sound of a door creaking had us shutting up and watching as she opened it a fraction. Her arm snaked out and snagged the bags quickly before the door shut once more and the lock clicked. Yep, that girl was gonna break my heart before this day was over.

Blade shook his head before he spoke in a quiet voice. "I doubt that girl's ever been allowed to be a child. She says she doesn't want to get handed over to parents who've already let her down in the worst way, and I agree with her. No way that's gonna end well for her. And I'm not going to risk her ending up like—" His voice broke, unable to even say the name of his lost love. "I just can't."

Arrow rubbed his jaw, giving his beard a tug before speaking.

"We can't have her living at the clubhouse. She needs a family to take her in. Keys should be able to sort out getting her all the paperwork we need to make it legal, but she needs somewhere to call home. She's going to be like Ariel in a lot of ways and is going to need that level of care."

Ariel was the little girl Scout and Marie had adopted after her mom died while we were rescuing them from the cult she'd been born and raised in.

Blade looked at me. "You told me your woman said to bring me home. Take her instead. I'll live at your clubhouse—if I'm allowed—and you take that girl home to your woman to take care of."

"I can't just make the decision, Blade. I need to talk to Zara, and Scout. Fuck, and Keys. I have no clue if he can get what we need done. She's not a stray dog we're taking in, but a person. There are so many damn laws."

Arrow interjected. "Good thing we got a lot of people owing us favors then, brother. Call your woman, run it past her. I'll give Scout a call, he can get onto Keys."

"Fine. I'll call."

I stood and headed to the back of the trailer, but as I walked past the bathroom I heard Sparrow crying again, so I stopped and knocked.

"Sparrow? You okay in there, darlin'?"

"I'm good, Mac. Just be another few minutes."

"Okay."

Rubbing a fist over my chest, I headed out the rear door but turned to face back into the house so I could see if she came out before I got back inside. Then I dialed Zara, making sure I used the secure app so we could speak freely.

"Hey, bunny."

"Uh huh."

She sounded tired and I winced at the thought of her struggling with her narcolepsy when I wasn't there to help her.

"Sorry to call you so early, babe, but I've got a situation I need to run past you."

"What's happened? Is Blade okay? Did something else happen?"

I grinned at her response. She was certainly wide awake now. I fucking loved her so damn much.

"Calm down. Blade's put me in a damn corner, but physically he's the same as last night. Here's the thing, yesterday we busted open the mob's whorehouse and freed all the women and kids tha—"

"Kids? There were kids there?"

I was sure Zara would be thinking back to the Iron Hammers' whore room she was put in when she'd been kidnapped and thinking of kids in that situation would probably be turning her stomach more than it did mine.

"Yeah, bunny. There was a room full of kids there. It was seriously fucked up. We got them all free and handed them over to the authorities to look after, but this morning we discovered one of the older kids had somehow snuck into the back of the van. She's real scared, babe. Her mom sold her to the mob to pay a drug debt. She's begged us not to let the authorities take her because she's worried they'll give her back to her mom." I didn't mention anything about her father. Zara didn't need to know that at this stage.

"What do you want to do?"

"Blade's agreed to come back with us, on the condition that we take this girl in to our home to look after instead of him. He's agreed to stay at the clubhouse so we can have room for her."

"Bring her home, Mac. We'll make it work."

"Her name's Sparrow, not sure how old she is exactly, but she's in her teens. She's a fighter, bunny. Like you. She'd been there a while but she was still fighting. She was ready to take all of us on when we first entered the room. Her knuckles were busted up like she'd been fighting. They didn't break her."

"Well, now you have to bring her home to me. Do you want me to talk to her before you leave?"

"Maybe in a bit. She's in the bathroom still. Fuck, she's crying, babe. Bank went up and bought her some cheap shit from Walmart and she's in there crying over it like she's never seen clean clothes before."

My voice was choking up but I couldn't help it. I didn't have to see inside the bathroom to figure out that Sparrow was overwhelmed to have clean clothes to wear. Bank's baby sister was a prissy little thing, so I was pretty sure he would have grabbed her some extras that she's no doubt in there struggling to accept she now owned.

"Well, when she comes out, you call me if you need to, babe. I'll get things sorted this end."

"Best old lady ever. Love you, bunny. How's Cleo?"

"Love you too, babe. I just walked into her room and she's looking much better this morning. Go get shit sorted so you can come home."

After ending the call, I headed back in. I'd just made it to the table when the bathroom door opened once more. She looked like a little mouse standing there, unsure of what she should do next. Before I knew I was moving, I was heading her way.

"Come on out, Sparrow. Let me introduce everyone."

"Is it okay if I do my hair out there?"

I smiled gently. "Sure, darlin'. You make yourself right at home."

Yep, kid was going to break my heart before the day was done. I led her over to the table.

"Men, this is Sparrow. Sparrow, the blond guy with the beard is Arrow. Eagle is the one next to him with long black hair, then next to him is Blade. Bank is the one who went shopping for you and Jazz is the one who donated his hair products."

The prospect's cheeks went pink as he lowered his head for a few moments and the others laughed.

"Thank you so much. I love the clothes and appreciate the products."

Her voice was quiet but everyone heard her.

"Here, darlin', take a seat and we'll get some food on the go for you. Want some eggs? Toast? Not sure what else we have. We can stop once we head out and grab something more substantial to eat."

She took a seat and after setting her new backpack down beside her, began spraying some shit in her hair and slowly brushing at a tangle.

"Whatever you have would be great. Thank you."

Eagle pushed back his chair. "I'll get something for you, darlin'."

Arrow caught my gaze and lifted an eyebrow.

"Verdict?"

"She's in."

That had him grinning. "Knew she would, brother. No way was she gonna say no. Okay, I'm going to go ring Scout and get shit started. I'll let you explain to our newest daughter of the club what she just got herself into."

Sparrow turned her gaze to me then stilled.

I returned to my seat next to where she was sitting.

"Before I explain, I want you to know we're not going to force you to do anything, Sparrow. This is your choice. Now, you said you don't want to go to the authorities here in L.A. Does that mean you want to leave the area?"

She frowned at me but began to detangle her hair again as she spoke.

"The further away I get, the less chance they'll find me."

"South Texas far enough away for you?"

She tilted her head and frowned at me.

"What do you mean?"

"We're not local, darlin'. We're members of the Charon MC, a motorcycle club in Bridgewater, Texas. I just spoke with my old lady—ah, my wife—and she's told me I should bring you home with me to live with us. We've got a ten month old baby girl. That going to be okay with you?"

She finished the knot she was working on before she spoke again.

"I love babies. Are you sure? You would just let me into your home like that? It doesn't seem real."

I smiled at her. "It's for real. We can call Zara, my wife, if you want to and she'll tell you the same thing." I sighed trying to think what to tell her to make her believe me. "The president of our club, Scout, together with his wife, adopted a little girl nearly a year ago. Her name is Ariel and she was born and raised in a cult where her mother was the only woman. I don't need to tell you what her mother was put through. Sadly, she didn't survive, but her daughter did and now she's a daughter of the club, a very well loved and cared for little girl. You come live with me and my old lady? You become a daughter of the club too. That means you have every member of the Charon MC at your back no matter what. Little Ariel isn't the only one who's come from a rough background. I don't think any of the club members have had an easy life. MCs seem to attract those that have done it hard. You'd find acceptance and understanding if you came with us. No one will judge you, I promise. But it's your choice. If you want to stay here and try to make it on your own, that's your call. Personally, I'd much prefer take you with us so I know you'll be safe. But I refuse to force your hand."

Eagle came in with a steaming plate of scrambled eggs on toast.

"This'll tide you over till we stop on the road. We didn't exactly stock up on food since we haven't been here long and weren't planning on staying."

"Thank you."

Her voice was so damn quiet. I hoped it wouldn't take her long to pick up some confidence around the club members.

"I'll let you eat in peace while I go help the others pack up, but you'll need to give me an answer once you've finished eating. We need to get on the road."

Zara

Since Mac had called yesterday morning and I'd told him to bring Sparrow home to me, I'd been flat out. With a lot of help from Donna, Keys, Silk, Taz and Flick, we'd converted our spare bedroom into a teenage paradise. We'd left the queen sized bed in the room, but I'd gone out and bought some funky but stylish bedding. I'd thought about painting the walls a new color but like Taz pointed out, we didn't have time for it to dry so we nixed that idea. Instead, we'd added a couple of posters to the walls, a nice comfortable chair with a throw rug and cushions that she'll be able to curl up in. A bookshelf with several books to start her off. I was grateful Mac had been able to give me her clothing and shoe size so we'd been able to go buy her a few things. We didn't go crazy buying a full wardrobe for her because I wanted to take her shopping so she could pick her own stuff after she had a couple of days to settle in.

Now it was getting dark and it was just me and Cleo, who was thankfully feeling much better. The new meds were working on her ear infection, and her reaction to the amoxicillin had nearly completely cleared up too. When I heard the sound of a least a couple of Harleys, I lifted Cleo from where she was playing on the floor and headed to the front door.

"Shall we go see if Daddy's home? And your new sister?"

"Dada dada dada!"

With a laugh at my little daddy's girl, I opened the front door and stood there watching the two headlights come down our road. Eagle peeled off first up his and Silk's driveway, then Mac was rolling up ours. Cleo started bouncing against me and clapping her hands while she babbled excitedly at seeing her precious daddy returning.

Mac killed the engine then turned his head to talk to the girl who was sitting behind him. She looked over at me, clearly nervous, but I'd seen the grin she'd been sporting when they'd first pulled in. If she was going to live in Bridgewater, it was a good thing she liked being on the back of a bike. I took a few steps closer to them but not wanting to freak out Sparrow, I stopped when she gripped Mac's shoulder and climbed off the bike. She looked awkward as hell and clearly needed some practice. Practice I was sure she'd get in no time.

Once Sparrow had two feet on the ground, Mac was off and made short work of helping her with her helmet before he ditched his and was in front of Cleo and me in a flash.

"There's my girl! You about done scaring the hell outta me and your mom, little lady?"

Cleo, blissfully oblivious to the fact her father was half-heartedly trying to scold her, did her best to jump out of my arms to get to him. Mac grabbed her and after giving her a little toss in the air, cuddled her close with a kiss to her temple. Once he had her securely in his arms, he turned and gave me a quick kiss on the lips.

"Hey, bunny. Missed you somethin' fierce." He pulled back and held his free hand out to Sparrow. "Come meet my old lady and our daughter, darlin'."

I smiled as the teen slowly crept closer to us.

"Hi, Sparrow. My name's Zara, I'm so glad you decided to come stay with us. The other women from the club and I have your room all ready, but if you don't like anything in there, we can change it. Just say the word."

Her mouth dropped open and she stood there blinking at me. My heart broke a little at her reaction to having her own room. I went toward her with my arms open

"Can I give you a hug?"

Her mouth snapped shut and she nodded, but didn't move. So I went the rest of short distance between us and wrapped my arms around her, pulling her in against me. She held herself stiff for a moment, before she tentatively lifted her hands and put them on my lower back. I rested my cheek on the top of her head.

"We've got you covered now, sweet girl. I can't promise your life will be suddenly all sunshine and rainbows, but I can promise you this: you will never be alone, you will never go hungry, and you will always have somewhere to call home and people you can trust at your back."

I felt her silent tears wet my skin through my shirt as I rubbed her back gently.

"C'mon, sweetheart, let's go see what you think of your new room."

Keeping an arm around her shoulders, I guided her inside our house. As we walked through, I pointed out where things were, then we headed upstairs with Mac following us with a very chatty Cleo.

"Here we are, Sparrow. Your room. Like I said, we can change anything you want."

She gasped as she walked into the middle of the room, then stopped to slowly turn in circles with her hands over her mouth.

"She breaks my heart more every time she gets something she should have always had."

Nodding my agreement with Mac, I dashed away the tears that were running down my own face as I watched her absorb her new surroundings.

"Mac told me your size, so we did a little shopping for you. Just the basics to tide you over until I can take you to pick what you want later in the week. I thought maybe you'd like a few days to settle into the house before we go do that."

She dropped her hands and bolted toward me. I wasn't sure what the hell she was planning before she wrapped herself around me so tightly I was forced to take shallow breaths.

"Oh, honey."

I wrapped my arms around her and just held her.

"My mama, my mama!"

Cleo's insistent voice had Mac and me chuckling, but Sparrow stiffened against me.

"She is your mama, baby girl, but you're gonna have to learn to share her with your new big sister. Sparrow? This is Cleo. She's a demanding little thing and once she gets used to you, you can expect her to start demanding all your attention too."

I felt the way Sparrow took a deep breath before she peeled herself away from me. I took Cleo from Mac as she threw herself at me, taking a possessive hold around my neck as soon as she could.

"Cleo, you going to say hi to Sparrow?"

Apparently now she had a hold on me, she was happy to greet Sparrow, because in an instant she gave the teen a big grin, revealing all four of her teeth. Sparrow returned it and reached out to run a finger down her cheek.

"Hey, Cleo. Oh, wow, she's so soft!"

I grinned at the awe in Sparrow's tone. "Yep, there's nothing quite as soft as a baby's skin. I nuzzled my nose in against Cleo's neck, making her squeal in delight.

"Well, it's way past this little lady's bedtime so I'm going to go put her down for the night. If you need anything, our room is up the other end of this hallway. If the door is closed, just give it a knock and we'll be right there, okay?"

She gave me a small smile. "Thank you. So much."

"You're most welcome, sweet girl. There's towels in the bathroom, so just make yourself right at home and we'll see you in the morning. This one gets us up pretty early."

We'd already shown her where the bathroom was so I left her to get settled in while I took Cleo to get sorted for the night.

"I'm gonna grab a quick shower before bed, babe. Let me give her a cuddle goodnight."

My body lit up at the thought of a sexy, wet Mac and the second he finished with Cleo I made damn fast work of the night time routine so I could get back to our bedroom and my man.

Chapter 11

Mac

After I washed off all the grime from traveling, I braced my palms against the tile, let my head drop forward and allowed the water to hit my back, the heat taking some of the tension out of my muscles. Sparrow's innocent joy and awe at seeing her new room nearly took me out at the knees. I wasn't kidding myself, taking that girl in was going to be hard work. At the moment, she was still in shock that she'd stumbled into a way out of the hell in which she'd been living. But she was a teenage girl, one who'd been hurt and abused. I had no doubt she'd lash out and have struggles. Zara and I'd have to be careful to keep Cleo shielded from any fallout, but I knew we could do it. With the club at our backs, we'd get Sparrow sorted out and living a happier life.

I heard the shower door open, but didn't move, waiting to see what my woman was up to. I'd missed her so damn much, I wanted nothing more than to spin around and grab her, but I knew she would have been missing me too and I wanted to give her a few minutes to do as she pleased with me. I was sure we'd both thoroughly enjoy whatever it was she was about to do, and my response to it.

Warm hands landed on my hips before they slid up my back to my shoulders. Her warm, naked body leaned against my back, her hard nipples poking me as she pressed in close and slid her palms around to my front. Opening my eyes, I watched as she moved her hands first up then down my torso until she got to my cock, which was rock hard and throbbing for her.

She pressed kisses to my back as she wrapped her fist around my length, giving me a firm stroke, just how I liked it.

"Fuck, bunny."

I shuddered as she slipped around me, sliding to her knees and wrapping her lips around my shaft before I knew what she had planned. The feel of her mouth sucking on my dick had me shuddering again. I shifted my weight to one arm so I could flip off the shower before wrapping a hand in her hair.

"That feels so *damn* good. Fuck, I missed you."

I started gently thrusting into her mouth, loving how she looked up at me with her sexy bedroom eyes while she took me as deep as she could. Fuck, she was hot. She had her hands resting on my thighs and when she started to move one, I clenched my jaw. I knew where she was going with those talented fingers of hers and I tried to slow down my body's reaction, not wanting to blow too soon.

She gently rolled my balls as she ran her tongue up the underside of my cock, sending another shiver through my body. Then she slipped a finger behind my balls to rub that small spot that would send me over the edge if I let her continue for much longer.

When she pulled back so just the head of my dick was in her mouth and sucked as she rubbed her finger over that spot again, I growled and pulled my aching cock free from her mouth. Leaning down, I hooked my hands under her arms and lifted her up before I pressed her against the tile. I dropped my hands down to her waist as I slammed my mouth over hers and she wrapped her arms and legs around me.

Without breaking our kiss, I lined myself up with her core and thrust home.

She threw her head back, hitting it on the tile as she clenched down hard on me.

"Fuck!"

I buried my face in against her neck, kissing and nipping at her until she relaxed enough for me to start moving. As soon as she did, I flexed my hips, pulling back before filling her again. Shifting my hands from her waist to her ass, I tilted her body out from the wall so I could go deeper on my next thrust.

I held still to take in how fucking sexy my woman was, all glistening as she panted. Her fingers dug into my shoulders as she arched her back, trying to push herself onto me, to speed me up.

"You want more, bunny?"

"You know I do. Stop teasing me, Mac!"

She wriggled again and dug her fingertips deeper into my shoulders. With a grin and a growl, I gave her what she wanted. Well, what we both wanted. I started thrusting into her again, taking her hard and fast. Bending down, I caught her nipple in my mouth and after giving her rigid little nub a hard suck, I closed my teeth down over the tip until she tensed and shifted her hands to my head, holding me close as she gasped my name. Releasing her from my teeth, I lapped my tongue over the mark, easing the ache before shifting to do the same to her other nipple. All without missing a stroke inside her tight heat.

With another growl, I slid a palm up behind her back, pulling her in tight against me and away from the wall. Then I spun and left the shower, striding over to the sink. Taking her mouth in another hard kiss, I lifted her off my cock, loving how she whimpered into my mouth as she lost my length from within her. Breaking the kiss, I lowered her to stand in front of me.

I didn't give her time to question me before I had her spun around facing the mirror. She automatically threw her hands out to catch herself on the edge of the sink.

"Spread your legs and hold on, bunny."

Pulling her lower half out from the sink, I lined myself up with her entrance again and thrust back into heaven. With a firm grip on her hips, I started pounding into her, loving how the mirror gave me the perfect view of the way her tits bounced with each of my strokes. Her eyes slid closed as her mouth opened. The tingles that shot down my spine straight into my balls indicated how close I was to coming but I refused to go over until Zara joined me. Slipping one hand around her body, I found her clit and gave it a flick before rubbing my finger around it. In the two years we'd been together, I'd learned just how to set off my love. And two strokes later she exploded around me, her rippling muscles taking me right along with her.

As I emptied deep inside my woman, I wrapped my arms around her torso, pulling her back against me so I could hold her weight up. Her cataplexy might have eased since she'd had Cleo, but intense orgasms still took her out. It was good on a man's ego that even two years later, I could still love my woman hard enough she passed out from the bliss.

Zara

I came to find myself back in the shower. Mac was holding me against him with one arm wrapped around my back as he adjusted the temperature with the other. With a hum, I nuzzled in against his chest as he walked us under the spray, where he made fast work of cleaning me off. Still enjoying the afterglow of my spectacular orgasm, I allowed Mac to maneuver me around until he had me dried off and under the sheets. Before he climbed in beside me, he went and opened the door I'd closed earlier. On his way back to bed, he gathered up a pair of boxers and slid them on before climbing in beside me.

"Just in case Sparrow needs us during the night. Don't want to scare the poor girl."

I smiled as I raised my hand to trace a finger down his nose then over his lips and through the stubble that was almost long enough to be classified as a beard.

"I love you so much. And I'm proud of you. Not every man would be so willing to take on an abused teen. She's going to need a lot of our love and care to heal."

He nodded before lifting my palm to press a kiss to the center.

"Back at you baby. Not many women would take one on either, especially since you hadn't even met her yet. After seeing where she was being held and talking to her, there was no way I could have left her to go back to either of her parents."

"You didn't mention her father before. What's the story there?"

He lifted his shoulder in a shrug as he pressed my palm over his heart and began stroking his fingers lightly over the back of my head and up my arm, sending tingles through my system.

"Not entirely sure. She told me he would rather see her dead than under his roof. And I told you about what her mother did to her."

"Is Sparrow her real name? Sounds more like a road name."

"It's her real name. In her words, it's another gift that keeps on giving from her mother. Poor kid. Keys is setting up paperwork for her, I'll ask her tomorrow if she wants a different name. She's got a clean slate here, I just hope she'll make the most of it." He sighed heavily before looking straight into my eyes. "How are you really doing? With Cleo and now Sparrow? You doing okay?"

With my heart melting, I leaned forward and pressed a soft kiss to my man's lips before pulling back to return my head to the pillow.

"I'm doing much better now. It's been a crazy week. My mood has been swinging back and forth like a damn pendulum. It wasn't until Donna mentioned that the shit that went down at the cafe might be affecting me that I realized she was right. With everything that's happened since then, I haven't had time to process it. Night before last, I sat up late chatting with Donna and Keys about it all and yesterday and today I feel much better. More level."

Mac leaned in to kiss my forehead, melting my heart for him.

"I'm glad you're feeling better. I didn't realize you were struggling with what happened. I hate I had to run off on you twice this past week."

I smiled up at him. "I didn't realize I was struggling with it, either. It was just sorta churning away in the back of my mind, I guess. And the club has been really great. Even with me cursing them out half the time, they still stepped up. Taz got us to the hospital, Donna got us home. And they all stepped up to help get Sparrow's room sorted out." I smiled at a memory. "Nitro had to force Cindy to back down from filling her room with stuff from Retro Funk. She was going to have that room kitted out like you read about."

Mac chuckled. "I can imagine. How'd you get her to back off? Aside from getting Nitro to physically remove her, that is."

"I told her I'd bring her in to pick out some stuff herself. I pushed the fact I wanted her to have a say in how her own space was decorated. Mercedes helped me get that point across."

Mercedes had been raised in a commune and hadn't owned much of anything before she ran away and found herself in Bridgewater. Of course now her man, Tiny, spoiled her rotten with anything she wanted, but she would never forget where she'd started life.

"Mercedes has agreed to help us with Sparrow. I think she'll be a big help with getting her adjusted to living here."

"I'm sure she will. We'll get her through this, and then Cleo will have someone else to boss around."

I chuckled at that. "I'm sure she'll have her new big sister firmly wrapped around her little finger in no time."

Mac yawned. "Need to sleep, babe. Got church tomorrow morning, then I'll be back home with my girls."

"Night, babe."

I leaned in and kissed him again before I rolled over and snuggled back in against him, relaxing into sleep as he wrapped his strong arm around me. The way he cupped one of my breasts in his palm as he slipped into sleep made me smile.

Chapter 12

Mac

Morning had come way too fast, and I was still half asleep when I got to church. Normally we held church in the late afternoon, as MC men weren't exactly known for being morning people. But Scout wanted us to report back to the club about what went down ASAP. Made sense. If there was going to be any blow back, it'd be soon. We took down the head of the mob and took out their whorehouse, which from the size of it, had to have been bringing in substantial bank.

Scout hit the gavel and silenced everyone.

"Mac? Get up here and tell the men what went down."

I strode up to the front and turned to face everyone, then I recapped what we'd spent our time in L.A. doing before moving on to fill them in on Sparrow.

Keys took over when I moved back to my seat.

"I've been monitoring all reports coming out of L.A. and so far there's been nothing about Sabella or his men. I'm not sure what that means yet. Either they haven't found them, or they have, and knew who he was and are keeping it under the radar. I'll keep watching and if anything shows up, I'll keep you posted. I'm also working on getting all the paperwork worked out for Sparrow to be legally with Mac and Zara. That's gonna take some time, so we need to keep her hidden away as much as possible till it's all sorted."

Scout cleared his throat, getting everyone's attention. "Just like Ariel, Sparrow's gonna need some convincing to trust us. I hear of anyone doing anything to ruin that for her, there will be some fucking harsh penalties, understand me?"

A whole lot of yesses and nods greeted the president's question.

"Right. We'll have a family barbecue this weekend to welcome her into the fold. I'll see what I can do about getting her a cut by then, but no guarantees on that. Mac, Arrow, Eagle and Bank? You four have the rest of the week off duties. You've earned it. So has Jazz, and I'll be telling him as soon as we finish up here. But keep your phones on and handy just in case something blows up with this Sabella shit."

He slammed the gavel down and then we were all heading out the door. After gathering our shit out of the lockers, we made our way out to the main room. I wasn't hanging around but I wanted to catch Taz before I took off.

"Hey, Taz, wait up."

He turned to face me. "What's up, brother?"

"Just wanted to thank you for taking care of my girls while I was away."

He gave my shoulder a squeeze. "Of course. We're family. I was glad to be around to help. I hated being left behind while you two were off risking life and limb. I'm used to having your six, man. But the fact I was here when Zara needed my help made me realize that by staying behind, I did have your six. By taking care of your girls."

"Damn straight, you did. And I'll never forget it."

I pulled him in for a back slap then released him.

"Well, I'm gonna head on home. See how Sparrow's settling in."

"See if Cleo's got her wrapped around her little finger yet, you mean."

That had me laughing. "Think that one will take more than one day. Cleo did not like the idea of sharing her mommy last night."

Taz shook his head. "I bet. She'll change her mind soon enough. She can't resist having another person to boss around."

"True, that. Love that kid, but damn, she's gonna rule the whole damn world if she gets her way."

With that, I said my goodbyes, headed out the door and jumped on my bike. Before I could get it started Keys came jogging out to me.

"Mac! Wait up."

I leaned back as he approached. "What's up, brother?"

"I'll be coming over in a bit. Need to ask Sparrow some questions to get everything sorted out. Do you believe Sparrow is her actual name?"

"Yeah, I do. She told me it was the gift from her mother that kept on giving."

"Before I get there, maybe ask her if she'd like a new name, yeah? Give her some time to think on it."

"I will."

I'd make sure that girl got the clean slate she deserved. I had no clue if she'd want to change her name, but if she did, we'd make it happen.

Once Keys headed back toward the clubhouse, I started my bike and headed out. Ten minutes later, I was pulling up to our house. I had to smile as I opened the front door to the sounds of Cleo's happy squeals and a chuckle I'd never heard before. Trust my little girl to be the one to get Sparrow to laugh first.

I slipped into the kitchen and wrapped my arms around Zara from behind before I pressed a kiss to the top of her head.

"Things going well this morning, babe?"

She nodded. "Better than expected. She's really good with Cleo. Baby girl adores her new big sis already."

I looked over to the living area where the girls were both sitting on the floor, Sparrow playing peek-a-boo with Cleo. Every time Sparrow opened her hands, she'd pull a funny face at Cleo, who clearly thought it was the funniest thing ever.

"I'm glad they're getting along so well. And I'm really fucking happy to see Sparrow looking so relaxed so soon. I'd figured it would take longer."

"She's only this relaxed around Cleo. The moment I'm close by, she tenses up again. It's why I came over here, to give them a little time."

I held her a little tighter. My woman's soft heart would be hurting for Sparrow.

"Keys is going to come over in a bit and talk with her. He needs to find out about her history so he can get the paperwork all sorted out. He asked if I could talk to her about whether she wants a new name."

Zara nodded. "Even if she wants us to keep calling her Sparrow, it might be a good idea for her to have a different legal name. Sparrow isn't a common name. I'd hate for someone from her past to find her here."

"Good point."

Zara had changed her name from Claire to Zara, which was her middle name, to try to escape the Iron Hammers. It had worked for a little while, but she hadn't changed her appearance or her last name, so it didn't keep her hidden for long. She also didn't run far. We'd taken Sparrow across two state lines, and she was young. She'd change physically as she grew older. I was hopeful if there were people from her past who wanted to hurt her, they wouldn't ever find her.

Sparrow

I loved playing with Cleo. She was just so bright and sweet and innocent. She didn't judge me or look down at me. Nope, she just freely gave me her sweet baby squeals and giggles with every new funny face I pulled at her.

Even as we sat around the table eating lunch, Cleo kept looking to me for more play time. After seeing so many kids in pain and hurting in that warehouse, spending time with Cleo was a breath of fresh air. Like, this is what kids were meant to be like. All carefree and happy.

I'd known her for less than a day but I already knew I'd do anything to keep Cleo safe and free to be as happy as she currently was.

As soon as I finished eating, Mac cleared his throat so I looked over to him.

"Sparrow, one of my club brothers, Keys, is going to be over soon to ask you some things. He's the one that'll be sorting out everything to make it so you're here with us legally. So no one can come in and take you away from us." He stopped and took a drink of his water before he kept talking. "He wanted me to ask you something before he got here. So you'd have time to think about it."

I frowned as I stared at him. I wasn't sure about trusting this new man Mac was talking about. My life hadn't allowed me the luxury of trusting many people. I trusted Mac to a degree, and the other men who'd I'd spent the past few days with on the road. But I wasn't sure about extending that to others just yet. Mac kept talking before I could think of some way to shut this conversation down.

"It's nothing bad, okay? You're safe here and we're not going to let anyone change that. It's just, well, this is a clean slate for you. A chance to start over and Keys wanted to know if you'd like a new name as part of that. Sparrow is pretty distinctive, darlin'. If you want, we can still call you that, but legally if your name is something more standard, anyone who might be looking for you from your past is going to have a harder time finding you."

Zara took over speaking then. "You'll be just like all the guys in the club, honey. None of them go by their legal names. Like, Mac's real name is Jacob. And my legal name is Claire Zara, but I use my middle name. So, you'll fit right in here if you do want to have a new legal name to protect yourself while we still call you Sparrow. If you want, that is. It's totally your choice."

As Zara got up and started clearing away the dishes and Mac took Cleo upstairs, I looked down at my hands as I started twisting my fingers together. Did I want a new name? I guessed there was a chance my mother might come looking for me. Did I want her to? She gave me up so easily, I knew she'd do it again if the situation arose. So, no. I decided I definitely didn't want my mom to find me. I knew my dad wouldn't come looking. According to my mom, he'd known exactly where I was back in L.A. and hadn't done a damn thing about it.

A knock on the door brought me out of my thoughts and I looked up but didn't move as Mac went to the front door and returned with a man I hadn't met before.

"Sparrow, this is Keys. He's the club secretary, and he's damn good with a computer. He's going to get you everything you need to live here with us." He came over and sat next to me, taking my hands between his palms to stop me twisting them together. "Sweetheart, you can trust him. Everyone who has a Charon MC patch on their back can be trusted with your life. I know that'll take time for you to believe, especially considering what your mom did. But I wanted to tell you anyway."

Keys had come and sat down at the table while Mac had spoken. He was older than Mac and looked rough around the edges, but his eyes were nice. He had gentle eyes and there were wrinkles around them like he smiled a lot. That made me feel better.

"Hey, Sparrow. Like Mac said, you can trust me, darlin'. I'd never do anything to hurt a child. Ever. But I'll do anything I can to help one. So, how do you feel about sharing some details with me so I can get you some paperwork done up to keep you here with us?"

I gave him a quick nod. "Okay."

Zara moved to sit down on my other side and when Mac released my hands, she took one to hold. The warmth from her skin flowing into my suddenly cold hand felt good.

"Thank you, Sparrow. You're being very brave." He pulled out a pad and pen. "Right, then let's get this started. What's your full name and date of birth?"

"Sparrow Cole. I don't think I have a middle name. My birthday is the nineteenth of September, 2002."

"Do you know where you were born?"

I shook my head. "I think it was in L.A. somewhere, but mom never told me where exactly."

"Do you know what your parents' names are?"

I hesitated. My dad's name would mean something to these people. They might forget their promises if they heard his name.

"My mom's is Sally Cole."

He nodded as he wrote it down and I pulled my hands away from Zara and Mac, using one to reach for my glass of water to take a drink.

"Do you know if you have any siblings?"

I shook my head again. "It was only ever me and my mom."

"Okay, darlin'. You're doing good. Can you tell me how you came to be in that warehouse?"

I took another drink before carefully setting the glass down.

"My mom likes to escape. Drugs, drink… whatever she can get her hands on. Any money we ever had went that way…" I trailed off as I got lost in my mind. Something that happened ever since those assholes started knocking my head around.

"Honey? Are you okay?"

I mentally shook myself back to the present to answer Zara. "Um, yeah. Sorry. So, these men came around one day and they knocked mom around a bit, yelling at her about not paying her debts. I was so scared. I was hiding under the bed hoping they'd hurry up and go so I could get mom cleaned up like I normally did. But they didn't go like normal. They came into the room and flipped the bed over. One grabbed me and I bit his hand and ran. I got out of the room but the other man was in the hallway and he caught me. I tried to fight. I really did, but eventually he hit the butt of his gun down on my head and I was too dizzy to fight them. Before I passed out, I heard them tell my mom her debt was cleared this time."

"Do you know how long you were held in that warehouse?"

I shook my head. "I didn't try to track the days in that place. Didn't see the point."

"Do you know what the date was when you got taken?"

"It was past Christmas but before New Year's Eve."

It wasn't like I kept a calendar to keep watch on the dates. Not like I went to school or anything that required me to know the date. I only knew those two dates because of all the shops and signs around the place.

Zara gasped and I turned to look at her. She had tears running down her face.

"Why are you crying?"

"Sweetheart, it's nearly the middle of August."

I blinked at her, frowning. I still wasn't sure why she was crying. She hadn't been held there for nearly eight months. It hadn't been her who'd had to fight every day, so why was she crying?

Mac cleared his throat and I noticed he had tears in his eyes too, but he wasn't letting them fall like Zara.

"Darlin', we're upset on your behalf. You were in that place for close to eight months, assuming you were taken last December and not the one previous. We care about you and it hurts us that you were hurt like that, especially for so long. Does that make sense?"

"But you don't even know me."

I didn't understand how they could care about me like that, when they didn't know me.

"In that room with the other kids, when they took the others and they were hurt, how did you feel?"

"Angry. I wanted to hurt them back. I tried to stop them, every time. I never stopped."

"But you didn't know those kids. That's how we feel about you, Sparrow. You're ours to protect and it hurts us that you were hurt when we weren't there for you."

I nodded, understanding what he meant now. I'd been protective of all those kids, and I hoped they were all doing better now they were free. I'd thought about sneaking a few of them in the van with me. But I'd known they wouldn't be able to sit still for long enough and we would get caught too soon and all be handed over to the authorities. Wrapping my hands around the glass again, I got lost staring at the water as I tried to get my mind to focus on the present.

Zara

I couldn't take my eyes off Sparrow. She was so young but had been through so much. Clearly she was incredibly strong to have kept fighting for so long. But no one could fight forever, and no matter how strong she was, what had been done to her would leave a mark on her soul.

"Did Mac talk to you about your name?"

She snapped her head over to face Keys from where she'd been staring at her glass of water. That concerned me, she kept doing that. Just zoning out for a few minutes. I needed to talk to Donna, or maybe take her to get checked over. Actually, that would be better. She needed a complete health check to make sure she was healthy. I'd noticed she favored her left arm over her right, too.

She nodded. "I want to be called Sparrow. It's the only thing from my past I'm keeping. But I understand the safety side of it, and I'm happy for Sparrow to be my nickname, not my legal name."

I smiled when she glanced at me, as though searching for approval.

"That's real good, honey. Okay, so here's what I think will work best. Those in the club already know the truth of how you came to be living here, and the club is real good at keeping secrets. As far as the rest of the world goes, you are the daughter of Mac's cousin. Your folks were killed in the fires in California so you got sent here to live with Mac and Zara. That means I can make your last name Miller, just like Mac, Zara and Cleo. We just need to work out a new first name for you. Any ideas?"

Keys was good. That story was believable enough to pass. Mac had been born and raised in southern California, and so many had already died in those fires this year, with so many more still missing that number was sure to rise by the time all the flames were put out.

"Would Jane work?"

"That'll work just fine."

I so badly wanted to ask her why she picked that name, but I kept my lips sealed. I did wonder if Keys hadn't already suggested a last name if she wouldn't have said Doe. If she did just name herself after all the unidentified female bodies that were found, it spoke volumes about how she saw herself. It also strengthened my resolve to help Sparrow become so much more than she ever dreamed. She was so young, she had her whole life ahead of her to do anything she wanted.

"Sparrow? Did you ever get to go to school?"

She shrugged at my question before speaking. "I went a lot when I was younger. But in the last few years I haven't been. Mom got worse as I got older and the more she used, the less she'd let me out of her sight."

Hopefully that meant she could read and write. I'd need to talk with Marie about what she did to get Ariel all caught up for school. Ariel was a lot younger, but I was sure Marie would be able to point me in the right direction to find programs I could use to help Sparrow.

The sliding door off the living room opened and Silk, Raven, Flick and Lolly came in. I guessed Eagle and Taz were still at the clubhouse. Which got me thinking…

"Mac, how come you're not still at the clubhouse?"

He grinned my way. "Scout gave me the week off to spend with my girls. Then on Saturday we're having a family barbecue at the clubhouse to welcome Sparrow to the family."

"Well, I'm going to get moving and start getting all this sorted out. Thank you for being so honest with me, Sparrow. I promise I won't let you down."

Keys said his goodbyes and headed for the door as I turned my attention back to Sparrow.

"Sparrow, these are two of my friends. Their husbands are close with Mac. They're not only brothers in the club, but the three of them were also in the Marines together. All three of us live right next door to each other."

"I'm Silk, I'm married to Eagle, who went with Mac on the run. He's the one with long black hair. And this is little Raven, who just got up from his nap so is still kinda out of it. He'll be climbing all over you soon enough, though."

Sparrow smiled as she said a quiet hi.

"I'm Flick and I'm married to Taz. He stayed behind to guard us womenfolk so you haven't met him yet, but he's easy to pick out. He grew up in Australia and his accent is still pretty thick. And this sleeping beauty is Lolly."

After she said hi, Sparrow turned to me. "Does everyone have nicknames?"

That got a chuckle out of everyone.

"Pretty much. MCs love their road names and a lot of the women end up with them too."

"I lost my parents when I was about your age and moved here to live with my uncle and aunt. Scout told me I was smooth as silk with the way I talked my uncle into anything, so I got labeled with Silky. As I got older it got shortened to Silk."

"Mine's really boring. My name is Felicity and it got shortened to Flick."

"Sparrow's my real name. Well, it was. Now it's my road name."

Just like that, she'd gone from calling it a nickname to a road name. Damn, but this kid was born to be part of an MC family. I just knew she was going to fit right in around the club.

"I asked the girls over for two reasons. One was so you could meet them and their kiddos, but the main reason was so they could give us a hand with your hair. Is that okay?"

She gave me a nod. "I'll go get the stuff Bank got me."

She trotted up the stairs.

"That Bank got her?"

Mac answered Flick's question. "We found her naked in that warehouse. I gave her my shirt, so that's all she was wearing when we found her in the back of the van. Bank offered to go to Walmart and grab her some stuff. Guess with him having a kid sister about Sparrow's age, he knew what to get. Man nailed it. She loved everything he grabbed, including some leave-in conditioner stuff for her hair. Every time we stopped for a meal or rest she had it out and was trying to detangle her hair. I suggested we could cut it short and she looked at me like I'd suggested we hack off her arm, so I'm guessing that's not a solution."

"She has beautiful hair, or rather, it will be once we get it all combed out."

Mac moved over to take Lolly. "How about I add this sleeping beauty to the one upstairs and grab the monitor? Then I'll come play with Raven while you ladies do your thing."

I moved to stand in front of my man, leaning up as I cupped his face to bring it down for a kiss. He bent down and took my mouth gently with his. I pulled back and smiled up at him.

"Best old man ever."

He chuckled at me. "Stealing my lines, woman?"

Before I could respond, Sparrow came back down the stairs with a brush, comb and the spray.

"Right. How about we put a movie on before we start playing hairdresser?"

Epilogue

3 weeks later
Mac

Thanks to a burst water pipe in the kitchen at the clubhouse, the barbecue to welcome Sparrow was postponed. Then shit blew up with Bash and his mother, so it got put off even further, but I didn't mind the wait. It gave Sparrow more time to meet more of the club in smaller groups. To get used to being free. To settle in here to her new life, which she had. I couldn't be more proud of her if she were my own blood.

Marie had helped Zara find the right people to see about getting Sparrow tutors who have her on track to be able to attend high school next year when it started after Christmas break. It was a pity she couldn't start at the beginning of the new school year, but she was just too far behind to do that. Six months wasn't going to be the end of the world, and if she still wasn't ready, we'd keep her with the tutors till next year. Neither Zara nor I gave a fuck if she was home schooled with tutors till the new year or next August. Either way, our girl would get where she needed to be. That girl had no quit in her.

When Sparrow wasn't studying, she was either looking after the babies or helping Cindy in her store, Retro Funk. Which was, conveniently, next door to Marie's Cafe where Zara worked and just up the road from the gym where I worked most of the time.

I pulled up to the clubhouse on my bike and headed to the door. We were having church before we had the barbecue. I'd come in early so I could be with Sparrow when she arrived later. This would be her first time at the clubhouse. Nodding to the prospects on guard duty, I raced inside and into the meeting room. I was cutting it close, getting in right on time but I hadn't wanted to leave my girls. I tossed my phone into a locker and strode into the room to find everyone looking fucking miserable. It was a tough time. While Bash had technically still been a prospect, he'd been here for two fucking years and was a part of us. It was always a sad day when we lost a brother.

Scout gave me a nod then hit the table with the gavel.

"Keeping it short and sweet today, brothers. Most of you were here night before last for the impromptu farewell for Bash. I took him to the airport yesterday morning for his break up north. We'll see how it goes. He knows he's always welcome here, but I suspect he'll stay up there. Too many memories down here for him to live with. I know we all understand how that goes."

There were murmurs of agreement around the room. "There's still nothing on Sabella in the news. Hell, there hasn't even been a mention of the bodies being found in that fire so that stinks of a fucking cover-up, but I don't give a fuck. You clearly got in, got shit done, and got back out without anyone realizing it was us, so job well done, brothers. One less fucker to come after what's ours. Now that's dealt with, we got other long overdue business to vote on.

"I'm gonna include Bash in this vote, just in case he does decide to come back to us after his little vacay up north. This vote is for offering a couple of the prospects their full patch. I'll say the name, you either agree or not. Bash, if he comes back to us. Who agrees?" I called out with every single other brother with a loud yes. That boy took a fucking bullet for Zara, he should have been patched in a fucking year ago. "Jazz. Yes?" Another chorus of yesses greeted him. "Good thing I already ordered their new patches then, huh?"

Everyone chuckled.

"We ain't done. Need to deal with Mac's buddy, Blade, who came back with them from L.A. He's done this club several solids in the past couple years, giving us information. It was thanks to him we knew what was coming for Silk. And now he's stepped up to help us take Sabella down permanently. He suffered a great personal loss on top of his injuries, and he's got a long road ahead of him. I'd like for us to vote on offering him a place here, as a prospect. What's the vote?"

I grinned at the round of yesses. I couldn't wait to see Blade's face. He hadn't been sure about his place with the club, about whether the brothers wanted him around or if they were just tolerating him due to his injuries.

"Prez? Can I request I be there when you ask him?"

Scout gave me a nod. "Sure, brother. And we've got one final thing to vote on. Bulldog, you want to start this one off?"

The older man, the club's VP, straightened in his seat, before slowly running his palms down the front of his cut, over each of his patches, before he spoke.

"I ain't getting any younger, brothers, and my arthritis is getting worse each day. Not sure how much longer I'll be able to ride." He stopped to clear his throat a couple of times. "It's been an absolute honor to sit here at Scout's side and watch this club achieve so much. And I intend to continue to sit in this room for as long as I'm able, to watch what we achieve in the future, but I've decided it's time to step down as club VP and hand over the role to someone younger, who'll be able to handle the workload better than I can. That, and I want to have more time with little Raven before I can't move enough to play with him."

I could tell he was doing everything he could not to choke up. Fuck, I was too. This was a huge decision and a big change for the club. As far as I knew, Scout and Bulldog had run this show for close to two decades, if not longer.

When it became clear Bulldog wasn't going to say anything else, Scout took back over.

"Mac, brother, you did real good up in New York, and again in L.A. You've more than proven yourself to be a solid brother and you've always had the club's interests at heart. I'm nominating you for VP."

What the fuck? Hoots and hollers rose up around me but I sat there shocked mute, barely breathing. This must be what all the cryptic comments he and Arrow had been throwing my way over the past couple weeks were about.

"Do you accept the nomination, brother?"

I cleared my throat. "Ah, yeah. I'd be honored."

This was big. Huge. They wanted me as the VP of the Charon MC. I couldn't wipe the grin from my face, even as my heart still broke for Bulldog. That his health was forcing him to step down from the role.

Eagle and Taz both slapped my back as Scout called a vote, which was a unanimous yes from everyone present.

Bulldog walked around the table and I stood as he came over to me. He held his hand out and I didn't hesitate to grab it. He pulled me in for a back-slap hug as he held my hand firm in his.

"I know you'll do this club proud, brother. I can retire easy knowing you've got Scout's back in the club and out of it."

"Always."

With a nod, he released me and moved away, allowing everyone else to come in to congratulate me.

Scout whistled, silencing the room. "Mac, getcha ass up here to the table. Taz? Go call in the prospect."

It felt so fucking surreal to take those steps up to the front and around that big table, to take my seat between Scout and Arrow. Brought a tear to my eye that I didn't let fall. Arrow broke the moment by slipping a VP patch across the table to me, along with a tube of super glue. "Get your old lady to sew that on later, but the glue should hold it fine."

I slipped off my cut and after laying it out flat, covered the back of the patch in glue before making sure I had that sucker lined up straight underneath my name patch.

Fuck. I, Jacob Miller, was now the vice-president of the Charon MC. I slipped my cut back on as Taz returned.

"Here you go, prez. The prospect."

Scout moved to stand in front of the table. "Jazz, welcome to church." He paused, grinning like a motherfucker and Jazz stood before him frowning in confusion. "Brother."

That one word made it clear to Jazz why he was here. You didn't get the title of brother until you were fully patched in.

"You serious?"

"Yeah, man. Just voted. You're in. A fully patched in brother of the Charon MC. We'll get your cut doctored up for you in a bit."

From my place up the front I could see the sheen of tears in the man's eyes. He hadn't been a prospect for as long as Bash, but it had been well over a year. It was well past time he got his full patch. I mentally made a note to find out the dates the other prospects had all joined, so this shit didn't happen again. We needed to keep a better handle on the process of patching in the prospects.

Scout spun and grabbed the gavel, hitting it on the table. "That's it, brothers! Church is over. Head on out and let's get the barbecue started! Plenty to celebrate. Mac? Before you go find your girls, let's go round up Blade."

Zara

Mac had gone in earlier for church. Normally, we would have gone with him but he wanted to be done with the meeting so he could be with Sparrow from the start of her first club barbecue. He was such an awesome dad to both the girls. Wasn't easy taking on a teenager. Especially one who had been so badly hurt. Sparrow had come so far in the past three weeks, but she still had a long road ahead of her. With the exercises the physical therapist had her doing, her arm was getting better. One of the beatings she'd taken did some ligament damage to her shoulder that continued to need attention. It had turned out the moments of zoning out she had were due to suffering too many concussions. Now she wasn't getting any more knocks to the head, they were getting fewer and farther between episodes. We were hopeful that in a couple months she'd be back to normal, but we'd watch for any long-term symptoms that remained.

I was extremely grateful that her nightmares were happening less often now too. I knew what it was like to wake screaming the way she'd done every night that first week. Broke my heart what she'd been put through already in her young life. Lucky for her, she now had a huge family to help her rise above it all so she could be whatever she wanted to be.

"Mom? Do you think I could come home with Dad? On the bike?"

My heart melted. Last week she'd started calling me Mom and Mac, Dad. Told us she didn't want to confuse Cleo by using our names while she didn't, since they were sisters. I loved that she felt comfortable with us so soon to accept us.

After lifting Cleo out of her car seat, I glanced over to where Sparrow was staring at Mac's gleaming Harley. I couldn't help but grin. Girl had it bad already. I could see she was going to be like Silk, riding her own bike as soon as she could.

"Need to check with Dad on how late he wants to stay, but I don't see why not."

It would mean a late night for her, but she'd sleep in tomorrow and be fine. Then, as though he had some kind of radar to sense us, Mac came strolling out of the front door, heading straight for us. He had the biggest grin on his face and a sparkle in his eyes. I cocked my head out of curiosity as he got closer.

"What on earth happened to put that look on your face, babe?"

He pointed to his cut, to a new patch that hadn't been there when he'd left home earlier.

"Bulldog's retired and Scout nominated me to take his place. I just got voted in as the motherfucking VP of the Charon MC, bunny!"

Before I could respond, he wrapped his arms around Cleo and me and lifted us to spin us around before putting us back down. Cleo was squealing in delight, and kept squealing when Mac pulled Sparrow in against him to do the same to her. Kid went red as a tomato at the attention but her smug smile showed she loved it.

"Congratulations, honey! That's huge."

I didn't bother scolding him for cursing. He was normally pretty good about keeping it clean around Cleo but when he was this excited, I knew he was going to drop a few bombs. Especially here at the clubhouse. Cleo was just going to have to get used to not repeating Daddy's bad words as she grew up.

"Dada dada!"

Cleo started bouncing against me as she reached for Mac.

"Hey there, baby girl. You miss your old man, huh?"

He grabbed her from me and threw her into the air before blowing a raspberry against her cheek. She squealed and laughed at her daddy's attention. He leaned over and kissed me before he wrapped his other arm around Sparrow and guided her toward the front door.

"Let's get the girl of honor to her party! Although, now you get to share the attention today. I wasn't the only one who got voted in at church this morning. Jazz is now a fully patched in brother and Blade is officially a prospect. It's a good day for the Charon MC."

I let Mac go ahead with the girls as I hung back, trying to wrap my head around his news. He was now the vice-president of the club. That was huge. If, God forbid, anything happened to Scout, he would be president. Whenever Scout was unavailable, decisions would fall to Mac to make. I knew my man could do it. He'd been a gunnery sergeant in the USMC, so ordering around a bunch of alpha males was nothing new to him. But that was a shit ton of pressure to add to his shoulders.

"Hey, babe?"

Mac had stopped and turned to face me, his eyebrow raised in question.

"I'm so damn proud of you, Mac."

His grin got even wider and he leaned back to give me a loud kiss.

"Love you so much, Zara."

Then we were back to walking into the clubhouse. As we made our way through to the backyard, Mac stopped and introduced Sparrow to a few people that she hadn't already met. I peeled off into the kitchen when we passed it, allowing Mac to continue on with the girls.

"Hey, where do you need me?"

The old ladies were all in full on prep mode. Normally I would have come in with Mac and would have been in here helping while church was in session, but Mac didn't want to miss a moment of Sparrow's first barbecue so we'd come in later for this one.

It took about twenty minutes to get everything outside onto the tables that the men had set up. Every time I went out, I'd looked around for my man and girls and found them happily chatting every time. It made my heart melt how the club was welcoming Sparrow. Not that I'd expected anything less. After all, they'd welcomed me and the other women who'd found themselves drawn into the club just as warmly.

Once the last of the food was brought out, I headed over to join my family. Cleo saw me approach and started wriggling against Mac.

"Mama Mama!"

"Hey there, baby girl. You done with Daddy already, huh?"

"Seems so."

Mac stole a kiss before he passed her over to me. With a small sigh, Cleo rested her head against my shoulder, shoving her thumb in her mouth as she did. She was nearly over her ear infection now, but every now and then still got a little clingy. I ran my palm over her head as I cuddled her in against me. Baby girl was getting tired.

Scout's loud whistle filled the air. "Quiet down for a minute. Got some shit to say."

His booming voice silenced the yard in moments.

"We've had a, ah, busy, couple of years and haven't done as many of these family barbecues as we used to. That's gonna change. Especially considering all the kiddos we now have in the club. Today's not just about catching up with family, though. It's about celebrating our newest members and the elevation of a brother. In case the grapevine is broken and you haven't heard, as of this morning, Bulldog has stepped down from being my VP. He's still a Charon brother and ain't going anywhere, but he's decided he wants to hand the reins over to someone younger. That man is Mac." Applause filled the air around us, making me grin. I turned to pull him down for a kiss, Cleo slapping her palm against his cheek as he did.

"Mac's done this club proud in the time he's been with us, and especially in this past month. I know he's going to continue to do us proud and be an excellent VP." He paused and cleared his throat. "While we're all focused on the Miller family, Sparrow, wanna come over here for a minute, darlin'?"

I couldn't stop grinning when I noticed what Marie had in her hands as she stood behind Scout, but from the shocked look on Sparrow's face, I figured she had no clue what was about to happen.

"Go on, honey. You're going to love this."

She looked nervous as hell, but when Mac rested a palm on her shoulder and started to guide her over to Scout, she went with him. Once they were in front of the club president, Mac stood to the side so everyone could see Sparrow.

"I think most of you have met, Sparrow, our newest Daughter of the Club. With that title comes a cut."

Marie handed the leather to Scout, and he held it up for her and everyone to see.

The squeal Sparrow let loose was pretty damn close to what Cleo sounded like. She slammed a hand over her mouth as her eyes teared up.

"Arm out, darlin'."

She put her right arm out and Scout threaded the leather vest over it. Sparrow turned and put the other arm through the other arm hole. Once she had it on, Scout's big palms covered her small shoulders, keeping them both facing out toward the entire club.

"Let's hear a loud welcome to the Charon MC for Sparrow!"

Everyone cheered for her as she dashed away a few tears.

"Row Row!" Cleo called out and Scout lifted his palms so Sparrow could come over to us. Mac had been right. Cleo already had her big sister firmly wrapped around her finger.

"Looking good there, kiddo."

Her cheeks had pinkened, and her eyes sparkled with life in a way I hadn't seen before and it made my heart melt for her.

Sparrow reached out and took Cleo for a cuddle. "Hey, little sis. Look what I got!"

Cleo patted the Daughter of the Club patch, a red heart with barbed wire wrapped around it that sat on the left side of the front of Sparrow's cut. Silk's cut had the same patch, as did any other woman who'd been raised in the club. That patch was special and meant that Sparrow was protected from here on out.

"We're not quite done. Jazz, get your ass up here, brother."

He swaggered up to Scout like he owned the damn world, wearing his cut with its new patches declaring him a fully patched in brother of the Charon MC. Scout wrapped an arm around his shoulder. "No longer a prospect, Jazz is now a patched in brother. You've earned that patch time and again, and I'm proud to welcome you into the brotherhood."

As another round of cheers went up, I noticed Sparrow cuddled Cleo a bit closer when Jazz gave her a wink before he strode off toward the other single brothers, where he got back slaps and was handed a beer. The whole time Sparrow frowned over at him. I bit my lip to stop from chuckling when she slowly moved away from me, in the opposite direction of the single men.

I hadn't been sure how she'd go being surrounded with so many males after what she went through. Especially the younger, good looking guys. So I was happy to see, although, she was avoiding one-on-one contact with the men, she didn't appear scared at all.

I'd noticed Jazz had flicked his gaze her way a few times now. Since he was one of the five who'd gone in and rescued her, he was most likely feeling extra protective over the teen. At fifteen, she didn't need to be worrying about boys, even if she hadn't been put in that damn warehouse for eight months. So I was grateful she hadn't noticed exactly how closely Jazz was keeping his eye on her today. Jazz was a few years older than her and in no way ready to settle down either. But you never knew what the future might hold for them. She could do worse than have a Charon man as her man.

"Stop it."

I blinked over at Mac as he wrapped his arms around me. "Stop what?"

"Marrying them off already. Neither of them is old enough for that shit."

A round of loud laughter drew my gaze back to the single men of the club to see them all stripping off their cuts and shirts before putting their cuts back on. I also caught Jazz pass another quick glance and smirk Sparrow's way as he shrugged his colors back on and tucked his shirt into his back pocket. He was a good-looking man, for a young guy.

Mac groaned. "Gonna have to have a talk with that boy. I didn't think I'd have to be scaring off guys quite this early."

I stood on my tip toes and kissed his bearded cheek. "With two daughters, you'd best get used to it, babe."

But I wasn't worried. I knew Jazz wouldn't try anything while she was so young, especially considering he knew exactly what she'd been through in that warehouse. And if they did end up together later on? Well, I was perfectly fine with my newest daughter ending up with a Charon brother.

After my chat with Donna and several chats with Mac over these past weeks, my swinging emotions had thankfully settled down. For all the times I cursed the Charon MC, it was moments like this that reminded me all the stress and struggles were worth it. Not only had they brought me a new daughter to love, I knew they'd keep her protected, just like they did with me and Cleo. If any boy was ever stupid enough to break either of my girls' hearts, the entire club would come down on them like a ton of bricks, whether they were a member of the Charons or a civilian.

All in all, this rabbit hole I fell down two years ago was ultimately the best thing that had ever happened to me, and I couldn't find it in me to regret a damn thing that brought me to where I found myself now. I had the best husband in the world, and two gorgeous daughters to love and raise. What more could a girl want?

Mac's arms shifted to wrap around my waist and pull me in against him. He lowered his head to my ear as his hand dropped down over my ass, to the bottom of the skirt I was wearing.

"Love you in a short skirt, bunny. Sparrow's got Cleo taken care of and I need to be inside my woman right fucking now."

With a chuckle, I pulled out of his arms and put plenty of sway to my hips as I headed to the door of the clubhouse. I knew he'd love the skirt, that's why I'd worn it. All these cavemen bikers seemed to like their women in skirts.

Five minutes later, I found myself up against the wall in an office, my shirt pushed up, my bra down, with my man's mouth sucking on my breasts while he unbuckled his jeans. Then he lifted me and shoved my skirt up my thighs, before he entered me in one stroke.

"Fuck, bunny. So fucking wet for me. Now this is how I wanted to celebrate. Fucking love when you wear that skirt."

"I know you do, that's why I wore it."

With a growl, he picked up his thrusts, shifting his hand so he could tease my clit as he fucked me hard up against the wall like only he could. I tightened my arms around his neck as I climbed closer to my climax. Then with another growl, he flicked my clit at the same time as he sucked hard on my nipple and I went flying, coming hard as he thrust up into me once more before he filled me with his seed.

Yep, my life was about as good as it got. Great kids, awesome man, epic sex. And I'd never been happier.

The End

Other Charon MC Books:

Book 1:
Inking Eagle

The sins of her father will be her undoing… unless a hero rides to her rescue.

As the 15th anniversary of the 9/11 attacks nears, Silk struggles to avoid all reminders of the day she was orphaned. She's working hard in her tattoo shop, Silky Ink, and working even harder to keep her eyes and her hands off her bodyguard, Eagle. She'd love to forget her sorrows in his strong arms.

But Eagle is a prospect in the Charon MC, and her uncle is the VP. As a Daughter of the Club, she's off limits to the former Marine. But not for long. As soon as he patches in, he intends to claim Silk for his old lady. He'll wear her ink, and she'll wear his patch.

Too late, they learn that Silk's father had dark secrets, ones that have lived beyond his grave. When demons from the past come for Silk, Eagle will need all the skills he learned in the Marines to get his woman back safe, and keep her that way.

Book 2:
Fighting Mac

She's no sleeping beauty, but then he's no prince - just a biker warrior to the rescue.

For the past three years Claire 'Zara' Flynn has been at the mercy of narcolepsy and cataplexy attacks. But after she witnesses a shooting by the ruthless Iron Hammers MC, her problems get a whole lot worse. She's now a marked woman, on the run for her life.

Former Marine Jacob 'Mac' Miller has a good life with the Charon MC. He works in the club gym and teaches self-defense classes - in the hopes of saving other women from the violent death his sister suffered. When the pretty new waitress at a local cafe catches his attention, he wants her in his bed. But there's a problem. She's clearly scared of all bikers. Wanting to help her, he talks her into coming to his class. Mac soon realizes he wants to keep her close in more ways than one. But can he, when his club's worst enemies come after her?

When Zara disappears, Mac and his brothers must go to war to get her back. Because this time, she wakes up in a terrible place... surrounded by other desperate women, and guarded by the Iron Hammers MC. Can her leather-clad prince ride to the rescue in time to save her from hell?

Book 3:
Chasing Taz

He lived his life one conquest at a time. She calculated her every move… until she met him.

Former Marine Donovan 'Taz' Lee might appear to be a carefree Aussie bloke living it up as a member of the Texan motorcycle club, Charon MC, but the truth is so much more complicated. With blood and tears haunting his past and threatening to destroy his future, Taz is completely unprepared for the woman of his dreams, when she comes in and knocks him on his ass. Literally.

Felicity "Flick" Vaughn joined the FBI to get answers behind her brother's dishonorable discharge and abandonment of his family. Knowing Taz was a part of her brother's final mission, she agrees to partner with him to go after a bigger club, The Satan's Cowboys MC.

However, nothing in life is ever simple and Flick is totally unprepared to have genuine feelings for the sexy

Aussie. When secrets are revealed and their worlds are busted wide open, will they be strong enough to still be standing when the dust settles?

Book 4:
Claiming Tiny

Some rules were meant to be broken.

After being raised in foster care, Ryan 'Tiny' Nelson has no plans to settle down. But that idea goes right out the window when Missy shows up at the clubhouse. One taste of the Charon MC's newest club whore and he's hooked.

Love is the last thing on Mercedes 'Missy' Soto's mind when she runs to the Charon MC for protection. But the first time Tiny wraps his arms around her, he captures her heart in the process.

When things start unravelling, Missy panics and runs. Will Tiny find her in time to give her a Christmas to remember, or will he lose her forever once her past catches up with her?

Book 5:
Saving Scout

Nothing worthwhile in life ever comes fast or easy.

Twenty five years after first meeting the Charon MC's president, Scout, Marie is still waiting for him to realize they're meant to be together. But instead, he comes to her asking she hire his ex. Frustrated with his continued rejection, she leaves town for the weekend to clear her head and maybe find a man who'll help her forget her infatuation.

When Scout first met Marie, she was way too young, and he hadn't been looking to settle down. Over the years, he'd never bothered to rethink his stance. When he learns Marie has fled town, he panics and realizes he needs to step up and claim what has always been his. Tracking her down, he approaches her at her hotel and he finally lets the sparks fly.

But before they can ride off into the sunset, trouble brews and Scout is taken by an enemy from their past that neither of them knew had been waiting for them. Can they overcome this latest hurdle to finally find their happily ever after? Or are they doomed to always be apart?

Book 6:
Tripping Nitro

Sometimes the one that got away comes Back… bringing trouble with her.

It's really her. Former Navy SEAL and member of Charon MC, Nitro can't believe his eyes when he finds his high school girlfriend in a bar nineteen years after she disappeared, taking his heart with her.

Alone and running from a stalker since she was 16 years old, Cindy has avoided all contact with the opposite sex in order to keep her mysterious stalker appeased. Now, with Nitro by her side, he vows to keep both her body and heart protected, but can she risk believing him?

With the help of his Charon MC brothers, Nitro keeps Cindy guarded while he attempts to woo her back into his arms. But just when he manages to break through her walls, she vanishes again. Will Nitro be able to put together all the pieces of the puzzle in time to save his first and only true love?

Book 7:
Scout's Legacy

***There's nothing he won't do to keep those
he loves safe.***

It might have taken Charlie "Scout" Dalton, the president of the Charon MC, over twenty years to see what was right in front of him, but once he did, he didn't waste a moment tying her to him. Now happily married to the love of his life, Marie, they were expecting a baby and had adopted little Ariel. His life was coming up roses.

Once ready to give up on Scout, Marie was now living her dream. Married to the man she's loved forever and carrying his baby in her belly.

But nothing in life ever goes to plan, and the birth of their baby is no exception. An unknown enemy comes to Bridgewater and chaos ensues. In the aftermath, Scout finds his loyalty to everything he holds dear tested. Will he be able to find a way to both save his club and be there for his family?